T0195027

MARLA

Story of a Cow

Diana R. Wright & Rita J. Cayou

authorHOUSE®

AuthorHouse™
1663 Liberty Drive
Bloomington, IN 47403
www.authorhouse.com
Phone: 833-262-8899

This is a work of fiction. All of the characters, names, incidents,
organizations, and dialogue in this novel are either the products
of the authors' imaginations or are used fictitiously.

Published by AuthorHouse 04/12/2021

ISBN: 978-1-6655-0745-5 (sc)
ISBN: 978-1-6655-0744-8 (hc)
ISBN: 978-1-6655-0743-1 (e)

Library of Congress Control Number: 2020922327

Print information available on the last page.

Interior Art credit: Diane Denghausen

This book is printed on acid-free paper.

I AM A COW.

My name is Marla.
This is my story.

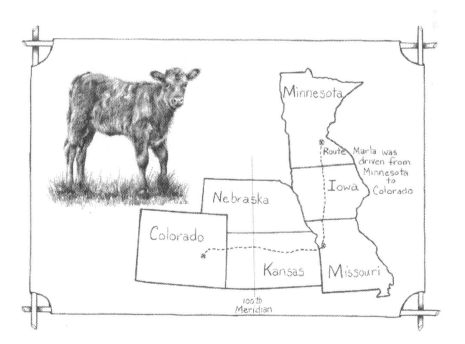

CONTENTS

ACKNOWLEDGEMENTS / THANK YOU

* Art Credit to Diane Denghausen
* Editing and compassion to Ann Swanson
* Endorsement to Dr. Bernard Rollin
* To the Love of my life for all the support, day or night, Dr. Bernadette DeCoke

NOTES FROM THE AUTHORS

This story is told from a cow's perspective but with great liberties taken to enhance and deepen the true understanding of a cow's life and the importance of relationship with and responsible husbandry by caretakers. Cows thrive or can be irreparably traumatized depending on the quality of care provided by the farmer/rancher. Beginning in Minnesota with one calf's birth, survival despite one of the worst winter storms ever recorded, Marla's story then recounts her arduous journey across the United States westward to the plains of Colorado and her acclimatization to the windblown and diverse terrain she encounters there.

Marla's herd lived on a small, poor dairy farm of 80 acres. The human family, the Olesons, claimed to have been "born into farming" and two generations had survived a multitude of Minnesota seasons. The third generation included the father, Bill, his wife, Marion and their children, Ben and Donna. Their farm was located south of Mille Lacs Lake. The Rum River equally divided the property. A dirt road bordered the farm on the east with an old wooden bridge tentatively poised over the river. Minnesota is east of the 100th meridian and averages 20-25 inches of rain during the growing season. It is touted as the land of 10,000 lakes. As interesting as that may be, it did not affect Marla's life there in the 1960's.

Though the story is a compilation of the lives of several cows, since the age factor between humans and cows is approximately one to five, Marla, a Brown Swiss cow, was real. The revelations regarding cow behavior / life and farming / ranching experiences during the 1960's told herein are based on the authors' actual experiences and observations.

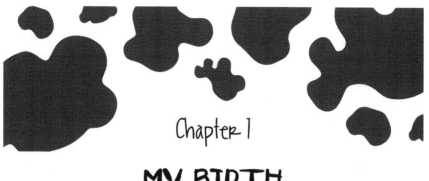

Chapter 1

MY BIRTH

I do not remember much about my birth, except the tremendous pressure forcing my head, front feet, and body through a restricted passage... then vast openness followed by a sudden crash onto something hard with dusty soil pushed into my nose and mouth. Suddenly I felt a burst of air flowing into my lungs–the first breath outside the warm cocoon. The air felt intensely sharp as it circulated in and around and through my air sacs. A cold penetrating chill bristled all the wet hairs on my small, frail newborn body.

Moist membranes covered my shape. Upon opening my eyes, I saw a flash of light and my first life form. It was huge, looming over me. I heard a gentle, soft "Moo," my mother's voice saying, "Finally you are here! I'll call you Marla."

Then, yuck! A swift force moved over my body surface. A rough, long tongue started licking me, pulling the caked dust from my nostrils and open mouth. Over my eyes and under my chin it swirled into my ears, outside and inside. Slurp, and another lick, this time underneath my belly and between my legs. I felt my body being lifted from the earth. Only gravity working in my favor kept my form to the ground. This seemed to go on forever, but my coat dried as my mother diligently cleaned me, her long smooth strokes invigorating my skin.

Something, a strong internal command, repeated over and over, "Get up. You must get up, drink, and follow your mother. Do it now!"

Blinking my eyes and trying to focus, I twisted my head around, looking, searching. My new world was brightly lit, and a warm breeze ruffled my newly dried coat. Tall stems of grass surrounded me, tickling my nose.

Continuing with a soft, guttural "Moo," my mother continued. "I love you, Marla. Please stand up. You are in danger unless you can stand and drink. There are hungry wolves only a few miles from us. I smell their vile stench and hunger. You must be able to run back to the protection of the herd. Have some nourishment. Suckle."

I shook my head causing my ears to flop from side to side. Thick mucus flew from deep within my nostrils. I moved one hind leg under my body and pushed upwards. I fell over on my head and rolled. Ouch! That really hurt. I shook my head again. All this was happening so fast. I wasn't cognizant of much, but instinctively I knew I had to get up. It took every ounce of strength to try and force my uncooperative life form to stand.

The decisive repetitive voice was telling me to try again. As I pulled my hind legs up under my feeble body my wobbly legs started shaking violently. This time I made it part way. My back half was standing. Well, sort of standing. I was attempting to organize my front half into rising when I fell, face first straight onto the compacted soil. A tear rolled down my cheek. Another effort. Another tumble. My hind legs splayed out behind my body. I rested for what seemed like seconds before trying again, as Mom kept nudging encouragingly. This last attempt met with success and I was standing, legs propped underneath me like stilts, but I was up!

My mother mooed with pride and gave me a huge slurp with her tongue, toppling me to the ground once again. This time I immediately rose and stood, tentatively fierce although with quivering frail legs. Some moments passed before I took that first step, then another.

My protective mother kept prodding me with warm, wet licks as she positioned her body for easy access to her udder and my first nutrition. Instinctively I tried to nurse, but something was wrong. I gave a gentle head bunt. Why wasn't I getting anything? Darn it, this thing was supposed to work. My mother moved ever so slightly because I was suckling her kneecap instead of her udder. Pushing gently, following the contours of her inner thigh, I continued probing, feeling with my nose and tongue. Something tickled my nose that was smooth, soft and pliable. Not quite what I was seeking but by reaching with my tongue and following the inviting aroma, I found four long teats. Selecting the nearest one, I reached up, opened my mouth, and wrapped my tongue around this compliant food source. I started sucking as warm thick liquid ran down my throat. My tail wagged furiously with delight as I drank.

Exhausted after my birth, learning to stand and walk, then that first meal, I needed sleep. Awkwardly I folded my legs beneath me and sank to the ground. I awakened periodically over the next three days, but only long enough to stand and drink. Each time I awakened, my mother was lying directly beside me or standing over me. I heard many soft, comforting moos as I rested. She stayed by my side, resting, protecting me, while going without food and water for herself for the first few hours of my life. Then she would venture only a calculated distance, weighing my safety versus her need for food. With each departure, I was emphatically ordered to stay low and not to move or respond to any sounds.

Mother said, "Stay hidden where I put you and you will be safe."

I was deep asleep, dreaming a cow dream when I heard a strange new sound which was a human voice saying "Get away, Susan. We are not going to hurt your baby. You thought you hid her from us, but we were watching."

My mother pawed the ground sending a firm warning and placed her head over my body.

Two young humans, Ben and Donna, moved carefully so as not to block Susan's view of her child, not to position themselves between mother and baby. They knelt down, without taking their eyes off the large defensive animal.

Ben wrapped his arms around my chest and rump, holding me firmly.

"Donna, where is the shot?" Ben asked quietly. "Give it to her in the rump. Quickly, while I hold her! We don't want her to cry or her mother will knock us into the ground."

Donna cautiously and gently pierced the skin injecting a protective vaccine under the surface.

"Now, Ben, it's your turn to place the ear tag with her number. Get ready to bolt because this forces a hole through her ear, and she will jump up and run. No way to hold her down."

I did not feel the needle prick, but the identification tag, with my birth date and herd number was a different story. I felt a sharp pain on my earlobe as the tool punched a hole through the skin and secured the plastic tag. I let out a calf bellow, jumped towards my mother, and as Ben and Donna backed away, I ran towards my mother.

Blowing out a hard breath, Donna said, "Wow, Ben, this is so scary, but I would rather do it than Dad. He gets so angry these days. How about breakfast? We could go shoot a squirrel. I saw one in the big oak tree. If you shoot and clean it, I'll cook."

Ben jeered, "Can you cook without burning it? Ha, that'll be the day! Come on! I'll race you back to the house!"

On the third afternoon, Mother gently nudged me and said, "We must move. Stay by my side. It's time to join the others for our evening meal." I was excited to see who the "others" were and skittered and bucked in circles around my mother as she steadfastly moved across the pasture toward a gentle upward slope. As we reached the crest of the hill, I stopped and stared in amazement. The "others" were like us.

A few cows with calves were in a grassy field and stopped eating momentarily to raise their heads as we approached. Someone, much taller than my mother, sauntered toward us as grass blades fell from her mouth. Mother told me not to be afraid because this was the leader of the herd, a wise and intelligent friend.

"Susan, so nice to have you back! And what an adorable baby! Did you name her yet?"

"Thank you, Frances, for asking. Her name is Marla. Also, thank you all for keeping an eye out. We saw you chase the wolves away from us. I knew they were coming from miles away, but if they had circled us it would have been hard to protect Marla."

Shy at first, the babies hesitatingly hung back, watching warily as

5

their mothers greeted my mother with welcoming moos, sniffing noses, and an occasional lick. One cow rammed my mother's side pushing her backwards until the role play of strength and supremacy was determined. This was the dominant animal who was so busy watching and maintaining order, mostly fighting, that she was not the leader.

As my mother yielded, they both went separate ways searching for the tallest green grasses.

I did not appreciate the miracle of birth until much later in my life when I became a mother, but it felt wonderful to be alive.

Chapter 2

SPRING

My mother was a dairy cow, the mainstay of milk production in the world, a sometimes-hard life but necessary to feed the population.

I was born in Minnesota in the spring of the year. Spring! Warmth, peace, and plenty of forage. Indeed, I was lucky. I was to run freely with my mother, nurse at will, and enjoy newfound life.

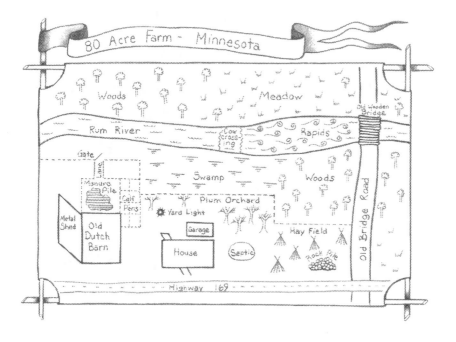

There were some other little calves with the herd. We didn't know why, but we were the lucky ones that spent the spring and summer roaming.

I was told that dairy calves are usually separated from their mothers after three days and the mothers returned to the milk line in the dairy parlor away from their babies. Then my mother looked at me sadly, saying that she was old, very old and produced so little milk she was cut out of the dairy line. This would be her last summer, which would allow her to raise me. It never occurred to me to ask where she would be going.

"What a traumatic time for mothers and babies," she said. It was hard for us to watch as the rest of the bawling calves were sorted off their mothers and run down a narrow chute into a holding pen. The mothers were pushed and prodded the other way, trying to turn around in the runway to rejoin their babies, to no avail.

At first the mothers would cry and pace, but the dairy line was their calling in life. They went back to their work in the milk parlor, twice or even three times a day. They would slowly move with the herd after milking and eventually stop looking back for their babies.

Their babies also cried and tried to return to their mothers, but they quickly became contented with a bottle of warm formula that was routinely brought to them twice each day. They did not miss the freedom they never knew. Home was a small pen with a sturdy shelter. It was safety to them, with soft bedding inside.

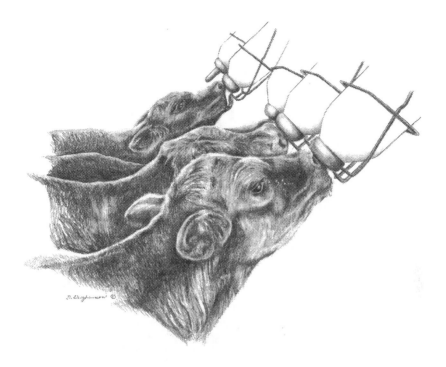

For the first week I was my mother's shadow, timid and insecure. I followed her everywhere. Then, with increasing self-confidence and strength, I started venturing out to smell the flowers and taste the grass.

One morning, a group of farm children led by Ben and Donna Oleson came walking through the fields. Their shrieks of delight carried across to the grazing cattle and every mother perked her ears listening for any sign of danger. Their senses relayed nothing to fear, only joy from these small visitors so they quickly went back to eating.

My curiosity was heightened so I cautiously approached while maintaining a safe distance.

"Oh look!" exclaimed Donna, the older of the two girls, "The flowers are starting to come up and, as always, the first to pop up through the soil and say hello is the Jack-in-the-pulpit.

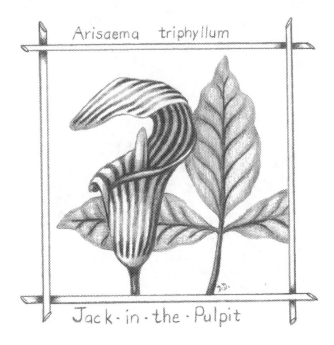

Arisaema triphyllum

Jack-in-the-Pulpit

How beautiful! It looks like a preacher standing at the pulpit with something important to say!"

Ben, the older boy, suddenly pulled his younger neighbor back, pointing to another plant growing on the ground. "Hey, Henry, stay away from that! It's poison ivy and if you touch the leaves, you'll get a terrible rash that itches for days." The other children nodded and moved on, boisterously exclaiming at the rainbow of blooms stretching across the fields.

A tiny little guy with blazing red hair picked up a rock and aimed it at me, shrieking, "You dumb cow, stay away from me. I don't like you. Get away."

Just as he flung his arm back, Ben grabbed it. He took the rock away and scolded the boy. "That's only a baby and she won't hurt you if you don't hurt her. Give me your hand and let's see if she'll sniff it. You don't have to be afraid."

The boy stepped back, pulled his arm away and said, "My daddy says cows are stupid and we should never touch them. I want to go home."

"Before we go home, I want to show you all something. It's called 'grub hunting.'

Let's find a friendly cow and see if we can feel bumps on her back. Then we find eggs embedded in hair on her legs. We must be quiet because the cow needs to stand still, very still because the eggs are so tiny. Ben got this eerie look like a creature on Halloween frightening the younger children and said, "The eggs hatch into larvae and crawl through the hair and burrow under the skin where they migrate up to their backs and swell up with pus until they're ready to burst free." He got the reaction that he'd hoped for with ill looks.

At this point Ben poked Henry teasingly, held his hand, and bent to examine a leg, getting as close as he could to coerce Henry into participating.

Ben turned and handed Henry to Donna saying, "Hold him up so he can watch."

Reaching with both hands, Ben squeezed a swollen mound of the cow's hide, and out popped a wiggling worm. Henry smiled, but the expression on Donna's face indicated a thorough repulsion.

Donna backed up and adamantly stated, "That was worse than popping a zit. Gross!"

Ben tried to explain to the pale group that these larvae festered, causing the cows to itch and be miserable. They felt relief when the worms finally exited their body.

He would perform this ritual as long as the children ogled and said "aww" and as many times as the cow would allow before she switched her tail, swung her head around and walked to a new area to graze.

"Doesn't anyone want to see it again?" he teased his rapidly retreating group.

Pushing each other, racing to see who could get to the old fence post first, arguing about who was the smartest, the children left us to be alone with the plant life.

With the children gone, I continued to enjoy these plants and felt comfortable watching them, not realizing their unfolding danger as one of life's lessons. The fragrance of the flowers and bright spring sunshine made for a wonderful day.

Another cow warned me not to eat the buds or leaves from the oak trees or acorns in the fall.

"You'll have a terrible stomachache, and start vomiting, and feel awful if you eat this," she said, stepping around the plants to eat the greener grass of the pasture." I fearfully bucked around her and ran ahead into the field. There was my mother on her way to bring me closer, lovingly protective, but with a scowl across her face.

Surrounding these flowers were the grasses, soft carpets of delicate fragrant bluebells, and white trilliums as far as my eyes could see. Trilliums, trilliums, trilliums! They stretched across the field and into a forested area at the edge of the grassy valley. It gave me a feeling of peacefulness to awaken from a sound sleep nestled amongst these fragrant and delicate plants.

In early spring I noticed that the creeks were meandering with the motion of slowly melting ice, releasing signs of life. Deep in the woods, where it was dark and moist, covered with decaying fallen leaves, grew the moccasin or Lady's slippers. These plants, with their large, ridged leaves and slipper-shaped flowers only appeared through the early spring.

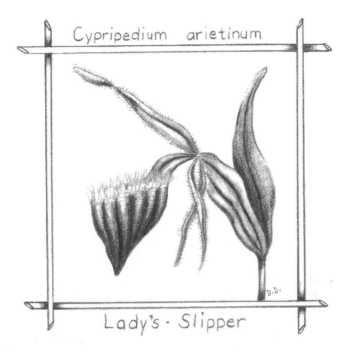

Cypripedium arietinum

Lady's · Slipper

Not everything about spring was nice. Biting horse flies had a sting unmatched, especially on tender young skin like mine. They were relentless and pursued their frail victims without mercy. Mosquitoes plagued us constantly as well, and our tails were put to hard use swatting at them.

One night, as I lay next to my mother about to doze off to sleep, the elders started talking about Minnesota winters being harsh, with bitter cold that could kill. Blowing snow left deep drifts. I didn't know what that was all about, but I listened. They said temperatures were below freezing and all animals suffered the ill effects. Spring was warmth, freshness and the pure joy of watching life unfold from its long winter's nap. My wise mother also said spring was a gentle rebirth of our souls revitalizing our spirits.

It took most of the summer to explore the various parts of the pastures. The land seemed expansive when I was so small, but eventually I discovered it all. We sniffed thistles, got burdock caught in our tails, and slept under the shade of magnificent old trees. Calves love to head bunt and frolic. Kicking at each other and then running to escape is a favorite youngster game. Playing hide-and-seek around the elders is another favorite. It was fun until we were told to stop and go play "over there" or under the tree, or just someplace else.

One balmy evening, after chores were completed, our leader stopped eating and began walking along the trail following the rocky river's edge toward the old bridge. That was all it took. One at a time every cow casually fell in behind her, telling the babies to stay behind for their protection. What in the world was going on? Quietly, we tagged along a slight distance behind our mothers.

The humidity was so elevated that all the farm kids had decided to meet at the bridge over the Rum River and go swimming. We watched as Ben and Donna jumped into the water wearing faded t-shirts and cut offs. Others started crawling down the planks, jumping into the cold water and screaming with shrill delight. Boys dunked girls and pulled them under the surface by their ponytails. Girls flirtatiously splashed the boys, attempting to look innocent in the process. The merriment continued for some time.

As we are so curious about human happenings, when it did not involve our welfare, we were lined up on the bank, single file, not missing one moment.

We heard a screech and watched as a rapidly approaching truck slammed on its brakes as someone jumped from the truck sharply yelling, "Get out of the water, NOW!" No one moved. The driver leaned back inside the truck, hooked up a spotlight and aimed it into the flowing water under the bridge. The people standing on the bridge, not brave enough to dive into the water themselves, became hysterical, shrieking, "Snapping turtles! They're swimming everywhere. There are dozens of them!"

We watched as sheer panic ensued with people pushing and shoving as they clambered out of the water to get on shore and back onto the bridge. From there they could see the many giant turtles with their strong jaws and open mouths swimming, just as in a synchronized ballet, gracefully passing each other. There was no aggression because everyone was having fun. Several people had felt "something" rub against their leg and assumed it was a bullhead or sunfish.

We watched until everyone was wrapped in their towels and on their way home. People passed on the story for many years. No one swam in the river again during our lifetime.

That night we all slept under the trees. The next morning, we set off to watch the dairy herd and quickly got back to the established routine.

My herd had patterns. We followed the same trail every day; but being small and having my own mindset, I would wander. My anxious guardian eventually loosened the reins and went about her way keeping a distant eye on me.

I soon became aware that a larger herd stayed in the next pasture and had no babies. I didn't understand why early every morning and late in the afternoon at approximately the same hour they traveled a well-worn trail. Crossing the river was hurtful for some of the elder cows whose long, untrimmed feet bruised easily on the rocks. They limped and struggled out of the water on the other side and ascended the muddy bank. They steadily made their way to the far corner of the pasture where they stopped. It was as far from the milk parlor as they could reach.

It was always the same. Early each morning and just before dark in the evening the humans had to go bring the herd back to the Dutch-style milk barn. Waving their arms with big sticks and screaming, they ran from animal to animal. Each cow would take only the necessary steps to avoid being hit. As soon as the human turned to fetch the next laggard, the first cow would stop and eat, waiting to be prodded the next few steps. This was a laborious process. It was obvious there was no cooperation between the two factions. It appeared to me that my elders got great satisfaction from this ordeal.

As the cows approached the barn they entered reluctantly and walked to their designated stalls. Each knew her place and most would enter, stepping gingerly across the gutter, placing her head into the stanchion. She would wait, switching her tail with anxiety as the human approached and snapped the closure, locking the animal's head into a stationary position.

The key words are "most would enter." The reality was that not all entered their correct stall. Instead of standing with their heads perpendicular to the head gate, on occasion one of the cows would stop, afraid to cross a shadow, or staring as a cat crossed its path, and would stand parallel, blocking the other animals from entering. This always caused total chaos and confusion. Bill would scream frantically, waving his arms and grab any close object to strike the closest cow. It did not occur to him to contain his anger and set an example for his children. Ben and Donna knew better than to question anything their father did because the screaming usually then flowed in their direction.

It was worse than their worst nightmare. Typically, every cow in the barn would back out of their stalls and run frantically down the aisle trying to escape. A large closed door at the other end prevented this. Bill, annoyed beyond his normal angry self, would curse loudly. With weapon still in hand, he would run frantically to get in front of the escaping herd. He struck any cow in his path. With seething hostility, he struck as many as possible, causing them to hastily back up. Eventually each correctly entered her stall.

They stood visually quivering as the head closure was locked. Most received a sound kick as he walked away, but the poor confused animal that had caused the initial turmoil was often beaten unmercifully. It was a miserable way to manage the herd, but as nature heals with time, so the gentle cows submitted again and again to the human's behavior although they never forgot the treatment in the milk parlor. Donna would get a brush when her father left, talk to the frightened animals, brush them lightly, and sneak them each a handful of grain. Ben quietly and carefully disappeared from the scene.

Grabbing a metal bucket filled with disinfectant and water, the human moved down the line and thoroughly washed the udders of the cows with a rag. His careful eyes sought out cracked or injured teats as he did this. Giving each teat a squirt or two by hand would show if there was any mastitis or blood red tint in the milk. Any cow that showed symptoms of infection was pulled off the line and penned separately for treatment.

After the human attached four suction cups to each cow's udder, the rhythmic sucking machine quickly milked them dry. When the udders were empty, the suction cups fell away. The actual milking process took around 10 minutes, just enough time for the cows to eat the grain placed by the humans in their feed bunks. At this point cows started to feel the excitement of being released back to the pasture, so they tugged and pulled their heads trying to free themselves while the human rubbed in udder balm on each teat to prevent cracking.

Bruises were not visible and healed with time, but poor udders effected the bottom line. Milk was graded and farmers were paid accordingly. Older cows could recite the routine step by step as they spent their entire life cycle in the unbroken daily pattern. This was life on a dairy farm in the 1960's.

"It wasn't always like this," Frances told me. "When Bill was younger, he and his father used to whistle and walk with pride, not hunched over like Bill does now. They spent hours caring for and grooming us. We were hauled to dairy shows and fairs. It never mattered whether we won or lost. Everyone was happy."

Chapter 3

THE HUMAN SIDE –
THE OLESON FAMILY

The Oleson family were of Swedish descent and had emigrated to the United States around the turn of the century. They proudly claimed they had been "born into farming," and two generations had survived a multitude of Minnesota seasons and hardships. They were not good money managers, but were strong, hard workers and family centered as they struggled to make ends meet in a changing world. As another generation began their working lives on the farm, the 'elephant in the room' was how long they could eke out a living.

Bill inherited the farm from his father, who inherited it from his father. Each generation borrowed against the equity to continue the lifestyle. They were not great repair people and the philosophy was, "If it ain't broke, don't fix it." Baling wire tied up most things and was used to fix fences, tie gates closed and hold the clothesline together. The modern comparison used to fix everything in today's world is duct tape. Where would humans be…

Farmers lined up used, worn out equipment in case they needed a part. Wealth was measured by the length of the row of used machinery. There was pride in saving and storing dilapidated "things", not indoors to preserve or protect, but outside in the elements. Rust was a patina farmers enjoyed.

Bill and his wife, Marion, had taken over after Bill's parents passed away, continuing the legacy of agriculture in the 1950's. It was a difficult occupation, fraught with the fickle Minnesota weather which could change in an instant, coupled with the dangers of working around hazardous farm equipment. Their livelihood depended on milk and crop prices being good enough to sustain the family and make money in the process. They were tough and resilient, but Bill had a bad temper combined with low frustration levels. Marion was the calming influence that held the family together, but she had a long drive to a demanding job which helped supplement the family's income. They had two children, Ben and Donna who grew up helping their parents on the farm.

While Ben worked alongside his father, Marion and Donna grew a large garden, which produced vegetables that were eaten fresh or "put up" and canned for the harsh winter months. The family took pride in being prepared for anything.

Then a combination of unpredictable weather, fluctuating crop prices and the cost of maintaining a sorely neglected dairy farm over several lifetimes began to take a toll on the family. A sense of frustration and desperation further soured Bill's outlook on life. These feelings bled over onto the entire family.

Bill sold some of the older cows, but the replacement heifers took several years to reach maturity and obtain high milk and butterfat yields.

In an ideal world...

Increasing helplessness gnawed at his guts. He grudgingly took a job driving a school bus. Chores were done earlier and later which extended the normal lengthy workday. It was an exhausting change for the family, but the thought of losing their farm took precedence.

One morning Marion peered out the window and watched as Bill trudged with his children toward the dairy barn. His walk was slower now, shoulders stooped in discouragement, worn coveralls showing worn patches. The children's clothes also showed signs of wear, but Marion was a skilled seamstress and mended nightly after the family had gone to bed.

They worked as hard as they could, but tempers were growing short as summer merged into fall. Marion knew they were hanging on by their fingernails. That deeply rooted concern caused a tear to roll down her cheek.

Growing up in the often-hard life of dairying, their son Ben didn't know what he wanted to do in life but was sure of one thing: He did not want to be a dairy farmer like his dad. He had seen firsthand how bitter and angry his father was and how his father took out his frustrations on the animals and his family. And yet his father, Bill, continuously verbalized the obligation of keeping the farm in the family. Ben felt guilty for not valuing or appreciating that family heritage, and secretly hoped his sister, Donna, would fill the role.

Ben and Donna loved going to school. Ben excelled at sports and charm, while Donna was on the honor roll and a leader in her class. Ben was personable and did not have to work hard with his schoolwork because he could do no wrong in the eyes of his teachers.

There was an unspoken rule in the school district that all students progressed to the next grade, no matter what their academic achievement. This especially applied to student athletes. No one would be held back because their team needed them. Ben had no incentive and his grades reflected his nonchalance toward book learning.

And there it was until the last day of school each week. Reality of life on the farm filled Ben with gloom; no friends, only chores and little time for creative play.

After morning chores on weekends, Ben and Donna had some time for themselves. They ran, giggled and punched each other, balancing on logs strewn across the pasture. They skipped rocks across the river in the quiet spots and threw sticks into the fast-moving currents watching them as they floated out of sight.

Many weekends Bill was too tired to help with chores, so they were left to Ben and Donna while he stayed in bed. The two children enjoyed these mornings because there was no screaming or brutality and things got done much faster. Then they would grab the .22 rifle and hunt for a squirrel to eat for breakfast, hoping that their father was still sleeping.

It was a clear day- no clouds, but a cooling breeze and the two siblings were off for yet another hunt. As they tip-toed through the grasses on the edge of the forest, taking aim at a squirrel sitting up on its haunches eating a nut, they heard a firm but soft bellow right behind them. Glancing over their shoulder, they smelled and tasted dust. It was caused by some large black animal, digging and pawing while stealthily creeping closer. They had been warned numerous times to be watchful and wary of this animal, but they had forgotten about the neighbor's bull in their pasture. Not hesitating for more than a split second and catching the bull off guard with their fast reactions, they charged over to the closest maple tree and barely made it to the second branch as the angry, thundering bull closed in behind them.

Knowing they would be missed, the children hollered for help, hoping their voices could be heard at the farmhouse. Two hours passed. They yelled until they were hoarse. No one came.

The bull bellowed and as his pent-up anger raged, he became so ferocious that he used his head to strike the tree like a battering ram. He did not leave his post. Finally, he lay down in a position to guard his prey and not let them escape. The children cowered on the branch, praying it would not break under their weight and that someone would come to rescue them.

Another hour passed before their father approached at a run. They heard him scream, "I'll be back with a gun. Don't try to come down!" He ran toward the barn.

They watched open-mouthed as their father quickly returned, squeezing through the fence, gun loaded with rock salt. The large, black menace jumped up to face the man and then mistakenly turned his rear toward him while bellowing at us. With careful aim at the bull's hindquarters, Bill pulled the trigger. The animal flinched as the load of rock salt peppered his rear. Tucking his tail between his legs, bellowing in defeat, he trotted off to be with his cows.

Crying, Donna sobbed, "Where were you? Why didn't you come for us? We were so scared!"

"Oh, I'll bet that damn bull won't chase anyone else for a while. He should have a sore ass", Bill said, shaking his head. "The Perkins family came over and brought donuts for breakfast. We started talking and forgot the time. Besides, I thought you two were doing some of the work that had to be done. It took us awhile to realize you were missing. I think you two learned a valuable lesson today."

It was some time before the two youngsters forgot that lesson, but after the breeding season, the bull was taken back to his home and the pasture was safe again.

It was common practice to borrow the neighbor's bull, trading breeding rights for the boarding cost, because no one ever looked a free bull in the mouth! Nevertheless, another lesson learned should be to check out the temperament of the animal to safeguard your family!

Chapter 4

SUMMER

The Midwest growing season is short; however, temperate grasses thrive in the spring. There was plenty to eat for all the creatures. Large oak, maple and poplar trees provided shade as leaves opened up from the warmer temperatures.

White tail deer, creatures with long skinny legs, beautiful large brown eyes and fluffs of white defining the edges of the huge ears, often ate with us. Like all of us, the scratching became desperate to stop the biting and sucking of the wood ticks and mosquitoes built like B-52 bombers.

Early mornings brought eerie laugh-like calls radiating from the river's edge. We saw a bird floating on the water's surface. This winged entity was not typical or cute like so many of the others. He had a shiny green and black head and wings speckled with white. We all laughed at the large webbed feet so unlike our hooves. Mother said the humans called it a loon.

Birds lived among us, sometimes riding on our backs, sometimes taking their meals in our waste, but always happy, always warning us if danger approached. They made nests out of many different materials including thistle down, weeds, and hair. Male red-winged black birds used the red patches on their wings to attract a mate. We did not understand this at all, but our guardians explained that all life forms were different and we should not judge. We should live in harmony and enjoy the differences. Those words taught us well.

Agelaius phoeniceus

Red-winged Blackbird

Summer days became shorter, and both the older adults, both human and animal, knew that fall was approaching. I had been through my own sad weaning from my mother a few weeks before, yet she remained in the pasture with the bull and other cows. I was now kept with other calves in a smaller pen.

One evening in late summer after the milking was finished, a human sitting tall on a horse rode out to my mother and the older group. Whip in hand he trotted to the back of the herd and began to drive them toward the open gate where several humans on foot waited. Flicking his whip toward the cows he shouted, "Get along there you old worthless sons-a-bitches!"

The whip snaked through the air with a hiss and made a crackling noise as the tip caught a slow-moving cow on her side, causing her to flinch as it bit into her skin. Startled, the cows broke into a rapid trot. The rider pushed them more rapidly now, and the cows funneled through the gate, continuing along the passageway beside my calf pen. Then they stopped abruptly while two humans fumbled with opening another gate that led to another small pen. As the cows stopped close to me, my mother and I stood together with only metal poles keeping us separated. Soft muffled utterances were shared between daughter and mother as our moist noses touched.

"What is it Mother?" I queried.

"I'll be leaving you soon," she confessed, her sides heaving from exertion and fear.

"You see, I am getting old. I have trouble walking and move more slowly than the rest. That is not allowed. You see how angry our human becomes when he must wait for me. You are a big girl now. You watch the other calves, listen to Frances, and please, stay out of trouble. Remember that I love you. I have had a long wonderful life. My only regret is leaving you before you are grown. You are too young to be without a mother. The humans will feed you, but never trust them. They can be cruel, harsh and intolerant." With one last rough lick of her tongue she murmured, "I love you, my child. Be brave. Be strong." She gave one last, loving moo as the gate opened and the rider crowded the cows down the passage.

Her friend, Frances, stood nearby full of sadness, head down, flicking her tail and bellowing farewell. "Don't worry, Susan, my sweet friend. I will keep an eye on her. I will do everything I can to protect her. Goodbye, my dear companion."

The cows were driven into another pen, the gate clanging shut behind them. Another human opened a gate ahead of Susan and the others, and as the whip cracked in the air, the cows broke into a panicked run and leaped into a trailer. The door slammed shut as the last animal loaded.

Susan was crying "Please, please, don't send me away! I want to raise my child!" These were the last words I ever heard from my mother.

The sound of the cows being thrown against the metal walls of the trailer when they turned the corner out of the driveway was heart wrenching, but the bawling and stomping noises slowly faded as the truck rolled on, pulling the trailer and leaving a cloud of dust on the dirt road.

A few days later, a new group of younger cows arrived at the dairy in the same trailer that had hauled away my mother. These cows were heavy with unborn calves and had a wild look in their eyes as they were unloaded. They all had a white sticky patch with a black number on their rumps that was pulled off as they passed through the gate into an enclosure next to the calf pens.

As they settled down, I moved nearer to them and they came over to touch noses and get acquainted. One of them rolled her eyes wearily and said she hoped this was her last new home. The barn and corrals they had been in for the past several days were muddy and smelly, with lots of clanging gates. Cattle were moved from one pen to another, accompanied by the sounds of human noises and trailers coming and going.

Another cow said she saw a trailer unloaded with several old crippled cows.

I stood and listened as the group exchanged pieces of the story. Even though the new group was exhausted, they talked and cried late into the night. Everyone had something to add. Someone recalled that one cow was named Susan and they revealed the horrifying end to my mother's life.

The story unfolded in segments.

They told me how the metal trailer gate opened and the cows, including Susan, stumbled out, running for several paces and breathing heavily. They were herded through an opening, where one at a time they were stopped abruptly by bars closing in from either side of their head catching and holding it securely. A metal gate closed behind to prevent them from backing up, forcing them to stop dead in their tracks.

Sidebars closed tightly and bruised her ribs as they squeezed the breath from her aged body. She could not move but urinated involuntarily while feces ran down her legs. She felt a tremendous force poke into her rectum, receding and pulling out feces, entering again and again. It whisked from side to side inside her body, searching in vain for a growing calf, attempting to determine if the old cow could by some strange miracle be pregnant. Nothing. Too old. Too late. Then a hand slapped a sticker on her back indicating that Susan was barren and of no further use. Our storyteller had personally experienced this, but fortunately for her, she had the beginning of a fetus growing, just large enough to detect.

By this time Susan was quivering with fear, enough fear to bolt forward once the door flung back. She ran wildly down a corridor into a stall that was covered in aging manure. After some time, another gate opened. Swearing, kicking, spitting, vile humans were all around. Susan was beyond terrified, but she continued forward.

As she passed through another gate, she found herself in a brightly lit small dirt-covered arena. Beyond the bars were more humans seated on levels of wooden benches. Some had white lit-up sticks hanging from their mouths, others spat tobacco juice onto the dirty floor, aiming at rusty tin cans at their feet. Occasionally the brown liquid even hit the cans, but more often it missed, leaving another splotch on the floor. There was so much smoke and dust in the hazy air that Susan almost tripped trotting into the arena.

In such a confined area, the smell of these humans with their sweat was despicable. Someone poked Susan's ribs to keep her moving. Everyone needed a good view. She got another harsh jab because she stopped to catch her breath. Loud noises, screaming, tossed trash, waving hands and loud bangs created by the pounding of a wooden mallet all contributed to the horrible experience. How much more could the tired old cow endure? Then the noise stopped, and another gate opened. Susan darted through hoping to escape. The gate banged painfully against her rump, making her hurry even more. Dogs barked and snapped at her already weak, bruised legs. The whip cracked and she ran forward, finding herself in a small pen. Susan was momentarily able to slow her gasping breath, and her eyes rolled in fear as she waited.

Two hours passed. Her erratic breathing had steadied. A small amount of energy had returned to her tired, worn body. She heard the distant sound of a horse approaching, the saddle bouncing up and down supporting a rider. The gate in front of her opened, but the thrust of the recoil nearly prevented Susan from exiting. She forced through with both hipbones scraping the rough weathered side boards as she fled. Frantically running down the worn path, the old cow leaped onto a trailer loaded with other older animals. Bodies were crammed together so tightly that breathing was difficult, and bones felt like they were being crushed. Then they heard the harsh sound of the metal trailer door closing behind them. It was dark, with only slits of light filtering through the hardened steel sides. They were terrified as they huddled together.

Suddenly there was noise from a starting engine. The trailer vibrated and moved forward. Rumbling down the road, black smoke poured from the tall exhaust pipes on either side of the cab truck. There was the sound of cows slamming forward and backward as the weary bodies were forced into the walls of the moving trailer showing no mercy for the hapless creatures inside. Then a sudden stop. More gyrating motions occurred as the trailer wove its way through traffic, causing even more pain to the poor animals inside.

The drive lasted three hours. Susan and the others ached worse than they ever thought possible. The vehicle finally stopped, and the trailer door opened. Exhausted bodies slowly funneled out into a fenced enclosure. Fresh water was available, but no one drank. They stood uncommunicative with heads down.

As I listened to the new cows' stories, I couldn't imagine the pain and terror my mother had gone through.

It is sad that as we attain our ultimate level of wisdom, we become old and useless in the eyes of others. It wasn't until much later that I learned what happens to cows after the trailers arrive at its destination with its old and crippled cargo.

Susan's final chapter of her journey was relayed years later, as it could have been told by so many processing plant workers and /or cows on their way through the food chain cycle.

Susan's story:

"A long period of time passed and my erratic breathing steadied. I listened as the noise of yet another horse and rider approached. This was to be the last 'Charge of the Light Brigade'. Herding us into another long channel, we slowed and stopped standing nose to tail. Inch by inch we moved forward. Then I heard a loud bang! Another forward motion. Bang! I felt a sharp thudding bump on my head. My legs collapsed from under me as I fell in a heap on the floor. My last distinct memory was the feel and sound of metal shackles being tightened around my hocks and a sensation of being pulled upward and off the ground, with my front legs dangling loosely.

I had no strength to fight or protest. I felt a sharp object whisk under my throat as a warm fluid began pouring into my eyes. Fading, fading. The pain was over."

Quickly and efficiently Susan's skin was cut off her body. Muscles twitched. A slit down the belly allowed her entrails to roll onto the ground. The processing plant workers proceeded with their jobs. The end of a life. Another step in the food chain.

I cried for days when my mother went away, but it was nothing compared to the overwhelming misery I experienced when the story unfolded about how her life had ended. Small and immature I could only imagine my mother's last few hours. I felt disgust and deep sorrow, but I had to go on and face whatever new paths lay ahead of me. She made me promise to never give up.

After weaning I was confined and alone in my small calf pen. I ignored the attempts of the calf in the next pen to be my friend. My mind traversed the pathways of the pleasant times I had spent with my mother and all that she had taught me. Roaming the pastures was now only a fond memory.

I cried until my vocal cords were raw. I lay down. I got up and paced. Not only was my companion-caretaker gone forever, there was no milk. My sucking instinct was at its height, but there were no faucets to nurse and no warm nourishment. I had no appetite and went off my feed.

I missed the wild grasses. I missed crossing the river and stepping on crawdads. I missed the feeling of being free, running and bucking across the pasture, with my head and tail high in the air. I did not miss the birds as they stayed nearby, always cleaning up every granule of grain that fell on the ground.

I didn't trust the humans who brought food each day. Ben came less often and as he grew, I watched his changes, now that he was a football hero. His friends teased him about being the star quarterback and he got to enjoy the flirtations of the young girls. His friends waved hats and spit in my direction trying to spook me. Ben only laughed.

It was Frances's regular visits that encouraged me to start eating. She came, followed closely by her child, tended to me and lovingly nurtured me as her foster child.

"Your mother would want you to grow and enjoy life. We will visit every chance we can. One day you will come back to the fields and then I will be there to teach you.

On an especially warm evening after chores, two tired men, Bill and the hired hand brought over two chairs and sat under the long branches near the plum orchard. The evening was quiet, and I overheard the entire conversation. They held small metal cans in their hands, from which they kept guzzling a pale, frothy liquid. It must have tasted good because they kept drinking while they talked. Every so often one would toss an empty can aside, burp loudly and pull another from a small twelve pack on the ground beside them. The pitch of their voices ranged from gentle to argumentative, punctuated by raucous laughter. Their conversation continued well into the dark of the evening.

Bill was grumbling, "I just don't understand these milk prices. They never go up, but the hay and grain sure as hell do. I asked a Director on the milk board, 'Explain milk pricing to me in layman's terms. I want to understand it.'"

He paused, rubbed his chin and continued. "That man said, 'We base our milk price on how much it costs to produce, consumer demand, and other factors.'

"'Well', I said, 'if your price is based on the cost of production, why hasn't milk gone up in the last twenty years?'

The Director grinned and told me, 'Sometimes one consideration cancels out the other.'

The hired man shook his head, saying, "Yeah and folks gripe at the cost of milk in the store. Wish they realized how much it cost to produce, and how little we get paid for our products. That'd set 'em on their ears, all right!"

Bill replied, "I keep telling my son, Ben, he has to take care of the family farm, but how does he make a living and raise a family? It just isn't right."

Finishing the last of their drinks, the men stood, tossed the empty cans into the box, grabbed their chairs and walked stiffly toward the house.

Chapter 5

FALL AND WINTER

I spent long hours, catching occasional glimpses of the humans scurrying back and forth.

They seemed to exhibit decreased patience, even with each other. It was evident that something unusual was in the air. The tractors were constantly in motion now. A mower attachment was placed on the back of one tractor. As it entered a hayfield, grasses were neatly and expeditiously cut and laid flat on the ground. Row upon row fell late into the night. Out of the darkened horizon, two bright beams came toward me shining so brightly that I ran into my small hutch to escape. The intense stream of light turned and moved into yet another section of the field.

While one small field was being mowed, another field was harvested. The corn crop was harvested and hauled in large trucks to long deep hollowed channels dug into the soil, leveled and covered with black tarps. This was fed to cattle during the long winter months, a nutritious but sloppy meal.

As the corn crop harvest reached its culmination, the hay was cured and ready. Baling machines moved along each windrow, a hinged piece of metal crammed the dried grasses into a compact square forming "bales" and machine-tied with a ropy twine made from the sisal plant.

Another tractor pulled a flatbed trailer between the rows of baled hay, with two humans on each side and two on the trailer. The humans on the ground tossed the heavy bales onto the trailer, as the humans on the trailer deftly stacked each bale tightly to maximize the load. The loaded trailer was then hauled into a covered shed. Sometime later, the empty trailer emerged with sweaty, grumbling humans sitting where the bales had been stacked. Late into the night, load after load was moved into the shed, until the field was empty. Each time fewer humans accompanied the trailer and every load ended with another worn body reaching the limit of his endurance. The next morning, the process started again. This went on for a very long period of time until the harvest was complete.

Frances told me that this was called "fall" and would soon shift to acrimonious cold which could be worsened by horrific winds. She told me to be prepared and to stay in the back of my hut. "It can freeze your ears off, but it doesn't hurt because they just get numb and slowly disappear. However, in the summer, it's awful because you can't wiggle your ears to keep flies away." She warned me to brace myself because winters could be long.

All the flowers stopped blooming and withered, the stalks becoming dry and rattling in the breeze, shaking dried seeds on the ground. Leaves began to change color from varying shades of green to red, yellow and orange. So many colors and all so beautiful!

One blustery day, I was quietly watching, peering up into the sky, when a leaf fell from a nearby tree and in its free fall to the ground, it hit the tip my nose. Ouch! The prickly end hit first and on the tenderest part of my nose, then sailed downward, landing near my hoof. I tried to pounce on it. Another gust took the little drifter to the end of my pen. It was trapped against the corner. This was my chance! I walked forward ever so cautiously, ears alert and head down, right up to the corner where it lay. Swoosh and off it went. I jumped back several paces and braced all four legs, stiffly waiting for the next movement. It didn't take long before my new plaything was in midair again, climbing and climbing and climbing, whisking from side to side. No! No! It was flying out of my reach! I hadn't had this much excitement for so long, I didn't want it to end. It gently floated over the rails that defined my space. It appeared to be looking back at me and laughing. Well, perhaps just a little smirk as it sailed away.

Momentarily I felt downcast. My leaf had landed some safe distance from my grasp and was just lying there. It must have been fate, as a sudden gust of air brought the thin paper-like structure back in my direction. It was set down outside my pen, but within easy reach if I put my head through the bars. I reached down and gently stuck out my tongue.

Surprisingly, the leaf stuck so I pulled it through the fence and into my enclosure. I bit down on it. Crunch! It didn't taste very good. In fact, it was awful, so I spit it back on the ground. The frail dry leaf was now fractured. I had caused it to break. This time I gently lifted it up with my mouth and took it into my shelter. I lowered it onto my bedding and lay down beside my silent formidable conquest.

As winter approached, the farmer's priority was the animals' feed. Without food, there was no survival for either species.

The second priority was fuel, and in this part of the country that meant firewood. It was free for the taking but required arduous and hazardous labor. Oak trees were a favorite as they were hard as steel and burned throughout the night.

Once the trees were felled and stacked in manageable lengths, a monstrous spinning blade was placed on the power take-off of the tractor. It took three humans to lift each log. The blade roared and screeched at such high rpm's that a 12-inch diameter piece of wood was sheared in half within seconds by the sharpened teeth.

Gloved human hands held these logs on each side of the blade, forcing them one at a time into the rapidly rotating menace. Speed was everything. As sections 18 inches long were freed, another human grabbed the pieces and tossed them onto the ground. Arms, hands and fingers passed within inches of the whirring piece of steel. Occasionally these got caught on a branch and were mercilessly severed. The unlucky person was snatched away as towels were fetched to wrap around the damaged limb, and the injured victim clambered into a truck that sped out of the driveway to the nearest hospital. It was fast, painful and bloody; but after some recovery time, life continued and the woodpile grew.

If the humans were lucky, all the fall work was able to be finished before the subzero weather hit and everyone would be well prepared for the mounds of snow and relentless blizzards. However, most years they were not that fortunate.

Howling winds woke me up early one morning. I walked out of my shelter and could not believe my eyes. All the trees were bare. Piles of brown leaves were blowing against the buildings and fences. Was this the beginning of something new or the end of something old? I had been feeling the change in temperature. My coat had thickened. I could see my breath in the frigid evenings. Life was boring, but I did have adequate food. My time was spent observing other changes and thinking about my mother. I watched as the soft glow of the yard light came on each evening and went off each crisp morning.

On most mornings the water in my basin was frozen. The first time I attempted to lick the water to get a drink, my tongue stuck to the ice. I jerked back, which was a painful mistake. Agonizingly, I pulled away, but some tender skin remained behind. Bellowing as the blood flowed; my tender taste buds were a reminder for many mornings. Some mornings I could break through by pushing my nose firmly into the ice. This caused my nose to bleed; but when it worked, the trade-off was worth the discomfort. Most often I waited for the humans to come and break the ice. They were my last resort as temperatures plunged.

There was no delaying the intense grip of winter that year. Winds blew fiercely. Calves near my pen lost parts of tails and ears, but Frances told me that it was seemingly painless. The freezing process engulfed thinner body appendages, numbing them. As these succumbed to temperature changes, they lost all feeling. Later, these parts just withered away and fell off onto the frozen ground.

A good year followed and several bad years- that was the pattern for farmers. There were too many variables. Bill finally had to get a loan from the bank to replace some of the decades-old farm equipment. The family's hopes rested on higher milk prices and good crops. They began sliding into debt as the cost of farming rose, and crop yield and milk prices flattened. Bill had sold some of the older dairy cows, but the replacement heifers hadn't yet reached their peak milk production.

The school bus income helped, but not nearly enough. Christmas was fast approaching. Somehow money needed to be raised to buy the children presents and to catch up on bills. One pen load of cross-blood calves had been saved just for this purpose. Hopefully, the sale of these animals would be enough to skirt another holiday season and get on with life. A large cattle hauling truck was called to pick up the animals three days prior to the sale. By hauling early, there was time for the animals to recover from the stress of the six-hour trip. They would have time to eat and gain weight before the auction. That was the plan.

However, there were many factors they did not consider, which is typical of small struggling farmers in a mass market. Prices in December are typically lower. No one wanted to winter cattle going into the harshest months. These calves were Jersey-Angus cross which were not a favorite because weight gain was not optimal. No one considered that the water at the feedlot might taste different than at home and the calves wouldn't drink. The auction hay was terrible quality with very little nutrition and the calves lost weight. They entered the sale ring so gaunt they looked sick. No one knew the integrity of the truck driver.

Did he haul these calves straight to the market or swap them for an inferior group? There was no way to tell. Sales were done on an honor system.

The nervous family had no way of knowing any of this. They waited with great anticipation for the check. Every day a family member would walk the tortuous driveway encrusted with snow to the mailbox, then trudge slowly back to the house, disappointed.

The day the check arrived everyone was in the house because a huge snowstorm forced all work to cease. The mail had been delivered. They were sitting around the wood stove trying to keep warm after Ben returned from the daily arduous trek. Wind blew through the cracks in the windowsills, walls and doors, whispering through the rooms and causing movement in the curtains. Bill and Marion inhaled with expectation as the envelope was opened and the check pulled out. With a sharp gasp, both adults fell back into their chairs as they read and reread the figures on the check.

Marion cried uncontrollably and could not be consoled, shoulders heaving. Bill's usual brusque demeanor worsened and he shouted, "Leave me alone! This is none of your damn business!" as he strode out of the room. The children's faces fell with disappointment while watching their parents' reactions. From the next room a safe distance away, he was heard muttering, "What are we to do? How can we go on?"

There would be no Christmas presents this year and only a meager amount to cover basic bills. It was a terrible blow financially, during one of the worst winters endured. If a harsh winter could worsen, this one set records--for cold, wind chills, height of snowdrifts, and longevity of storms. It was the coldest winter for many, many years. Ducks, sitting on their feet to lift themselves off the ice would stick to the frozen water. Their webbed feet froze and broke off as the birds tried to move. Newborn calves caught pneumonia and died. Their bodies were thrown on the manure pile behind the barn. Snowdrifts were 14 feet tall and shifted positions with the moods of the wind.

Farm families were isolated from everyone and everything. Groceries were in low supply as roads were blocked by the drifting snow. Hundreds of gallons of milk were poured on the ground because the roads were impassable for the trucks to come in and pick up the milk cans. Cows still needed to be milked two or three times daily. Families depending on wood for heat could not replenish dwindling supplies. Trees and dead wood were protectively buried. Homes were maintained at survival levels. Humans layered their clothing and went about their daily business, their frozen breath trailing behind them. Families huddled together under mounds of blankets. Meals were sparse but at least they had an adequate supply of meat, milk and whatever canned goods, as well as the garden vegetables they had put up the previous summer. Other food stuffs could not be purchased until the roads were plowed out, and that could take until spring.

As hard as the cold winter was on humans, it was worse on the livestock. Animals that were not protected from the cold or snowy winds lost weight at staggering rates. Many did not survive. Too many were caught in shifting snowdrifts and were left to die. One storm was especially cruel because the Olesons went out and tried to free the exhausted animal bodies trapped in deep drifts. Digging through the snow, Bill tripped over a barely warm carcass. It was Frances, my mentor and friend, with her frozen baby nestled in beside her thin cadaver--protected from the wind, but not the extreme cold. In the distance another weak moo was heard. The humans spent every ounce of energy fighting to save their animals. Some were saved. Some were not. It was a cruel winter.

Many animals died that winter. Their stiff, cold bodies were thrown behind the barn on the manure pile. Carcasses were heaped but did not decompose. Cold refrigeration kept the bodies in a suspended state.

Each animal appeared to be sleeping uncomfortably. Stiff bodies with twisted necks were lying on top of other bodies, stacked like cordwood.

Totally exhausted, the humans made it back to the house and pushed open the kitchen door. A gust of frigid wind caught the door and slammed the it back against the wall, leaving snow swirling into the house. A man's strong arm shoved it closed. With one last effort to pull off wet clothes, frostbitten fingers and toes started to thaw. The pain was excruciating. The glowing heat of the wood burning stove was a welcome relief, as was the large coffee pot percolating on the stove. The strong, hot brew warmed the insides of the family.

Economic conditions continued to decline as one bad effect compounded others. In the cold, cows' milk production went down. There was less money to buy feed for the livestock. The thin, frail bodies of the cows needed more nourishment just to survive under these extremes. They got much less. Farmers had to buy extra cattle feed since their own supplies were depleted with every cold day. There was no money so the cheapest, poorest quality hay was bartered--nor could they pay in the spring.

Grain, which is considered by cows to be dessert, was moldy and scarce. Morsels were distributed among huge herds. Bovines can withstand harsh conditions and have for many centuries. However, we do not do well when our stomachs are empty. Crying was endless, a deafening sound. There were screaming moos day and night, echoing over the countryside. I watched quietly from a corner of my pen as Bill Oleson walked by one afternoon. He tripped and fell in a mound of snow with a grunt of pain. All the animals on the farm knew that when he was angry, someone paid. Bill had become his father carrying all the anger forward. They usually feared his temper, but not today. As he fell into the snowdrift, he rolled over onto his back, crying out in anguish, "I can NOT go on! I can't listen to their cries any longer. God help me, please! I cannot go on..."

The worn body sat quietly in the quilt of snow for many minutes. As tears streamed down his face and froze into icy trails on his ruddy skin, I felt an unusual sadness. I stared in disbelief. I had never seen him slow down, let alone show any softness in his face. I waited apprehensively. It made me nervous that he was so close for so long. As he rose onto his elbow, I flinched with fear. Cold and wind forced him to get up and continue. As he walked away, I was overwhelmed with relief.

This human, so cruel, so calloused and so hateful after many years of work he never liked, was near a breaking point. He farmed because his father and grandfather farmed. He was raised to tend livestock and soil. He was taught how to milk cows when he was six years old. The first time he approached a cow with a milk pail he got kicked across the alleyway. It all started then, this growing anger and frustration that consumed him. Early, during Bill's school days and while he was in 4-H, he enjoyed the interaction and felt satisfaction working with the cattle. But he wasn't exposed to the financial end. He didn't appreciate that farming was not only a way of life, but a business that had to be managed.

Now he ran the family farm. He wasn't trained to do anything else. His formal education was limited. He farmed like his ancestors before him had farmed, never considering newer methods. Attending agriculture meetings just wasted precious time. Bill's energy was too depleted to read farm journals and why would he waste time trying any of these new ways? He didn't know the people who conducted all these new studies on farm management. Besides, they had college educations and his jealousy kept him from seeing any wisdom from the advice of these experts. He had watched his grandfather and father and learned from them but didn't see change as beneficial. Wasn't that enough?

Spring came slowly to the country. It started with a few drips of melting snow. Each day became warmer by just a few degrees. I was extremely thin but had survived. A blade of grass peeked up from under the mud and many replications of these small green tufts pushed with all their might and formed a soft carpet over the land. Dormant plants awakened to become sleeping giants, ever so hesitant, but once they were sure, their growth was rapid and sustained. As the grasses grew and were consumed by the cattle, fat began filling out the bony structures. It was difficult for me to forget the haunting memories of my friends being pulled out of their pens, stiff and dead. It was not easy, but I was glad to be alive!

The spring and summer were filled with activity. Recovery was a busy time. We lounged in the pasture, walked across the river, stopped by the meadows, and enjoyed the shade provided by the woods. We rubbed and scratched against the trees to rid ourselves of our winter coats, our tufts of old hair accumulating on every low branch. It was as if memories faded with the removal of this thick coat. Scratching brought relief. We rubbed until our hides were bare and calloused. We rubbed until we bled. Eventually new hair grew. It was thin and fine and felt good. It meant our bodies were healing.

As mothers gave birth, the welcome sight of newborn babies began dotting the pastures, and the process of weaning and going back on the milking line continued as it had for generations. The renewal of life, growth, and change surged with the warm weather. However, there were many conversations now about the future of the farm between Bill and his family which often included neighbors and friends. There were many sleepless nights until, at long last, a decision was made. Phone calls were made to schedule the event. Dark clouds moved overhead allowing second thoughts and changes in direction. It was agonizing until the contract was signed and the family had one choice, to continue forward. There was a final conversation with a close friend that provided the couple with compelling thoughts. "How many generations have you been doing this?" he asked. "What was your debt load when you started and what is your debt load now? Are you going forward or backward? Is this worry making your life easier? Life is short as you both know from your parents' deaths at such young ages. Are you able to move forward?"

CHAPTER 6

THE AUCTION

All of the cattle were improving and healing after the hard winter, but the humans did not show similar signs of recovery. Their expressions reflected doom, exhaustion, and misery. Although they loved the country life and were afraid to do anything else, it was time for change. Amidst raised voices, slammed doors and vehicles roaring up and down the rutted driveway, the milking and chores still got done, but there was a finality to things now.

The frustration of keeping the place after generations of farming became too much to bear, and the decision had agonizingly been made to sell out. Mentally, dark clouds moved through their minds, allowing second thoughts and changes in direction. Farm auctions are prearranged months in advance. Phone calls were made to schedule the event. All equipment, livestock, household items and miscellaneous things must be listed and organized. The category "miscellaneous" is a catchall term, which can include precious heirloom antiques, well used dishware, and the family's treasures mixed in with what may be deemed by the bidders as "a whole lot of trash."

A wide variety of people attend these events. Antique buyers hurry down the rows, scouting and noting the valuables. City folks mill around with ranchers and farmers, the city people decked out in new designer duds, with the country folks dressed in chore attire because the milking took longer than expected. This is quite an event for everyone and amusing for the spectators, the buyers, browsers and bargain hunters.

To the general public, a farm auction is a form of entertainment and holds the allure of finding a hidden bargain. For the family, selling everything is pure agony and misery. No matter how many times they try to convince themselves this is for the best, there is still doubt. Farms can be sold due to divorce, death, financial necessity or retirement. The latter word is just a polite phrase for being too damn old and tired to go on. In all of these situations it is the end of an era, a sad ending with little consolation for beginning a new chapter.

Auctions are planned for maximum crowd turnout. "Pick a day, any day..." is suggested by enterprising auctioneers. Weekends are preferred and with nice weather, especially those warm, slightly breezy days (not too hot) and never during a rain, wind or snowstorm. That's why there are "rain dates" on the auction flyer, a Plan B for the sellers. Of course, the complicated part of this idea is planning months in advance. This is similar to planning the annual family picnic so everyone can attend. Thus the auction date is carefully and thoughtfully chosen.

Flyers are printed up and distributed and ads are placed in local papers for maximum exposure. Equipment is cleaned, greased and placed in neatly aligned rows for easy inspection. Cows are groomed. Pigs are given fresh bedding. Water tanks are cleaned and fences are mended. Old tools are soaked in oil in an attempt to remove the rust. Of course, rusty items could bring more money because some people think they must be bonafide antiques. All the different motives and greed are what a successful farm auction is about.

The day had been selected. Arrangements began. The Olesons were selling everything including the kitchen sink and the whole family farm. As the day grew closer, activity intensified.

My counterparts and I knew something was amiss. We sensed

an even more heightened tension within the human family. Different groups of people now walked through the fields looking, pointing, whispering and sometimes laughing. The day before the auction, the animals were locked in enclosures with fresh hay and clean water. Special feed had been given to older, thin animals to fatten them up, feet were trimmed, shots were measured and given and hair was clipped and sheared to display the animals to their best advantage. Numbers were placed on everything including the animals, with numbered tags glued to our rumps.

One day I overheard Bill and Marion talking together. He said, "I want us to start over in California, a new beginning. We can get jobs, maybe with one of the aircraft companies. It was on the news last week that they're hiring. Can you imagine working an 8 to 5 workday and having every weekend off?"

Marion answered with some optimism in her voice, "Maybe this is for the best and we can find a house near the beach. The children need some fun in their life and choices to pursue advanced education, so they don't have to work as hard as we did."

Bill bitterly replied, "The sooner I never see another animal, the happier I'll be- especially those damn cows. I hate the whole life!" A tear rolled down his cheek, which he hastily brushed away.

Looking around fearfully, Marion agreed saying, "I'm scared, too, but I admit I *will* miss this place. This has been our life. Do you think we're too Hicksville to change?"

In spite of the careful planning, the day of the sale was cloudy and rain was predicted. It was scheduled to start at 9 a.m. on Saturday morning. Signs had been placed at the crossroads with colorful flags on tall poles decorating both sides of the driveway.

Cars, trucks and trailers turned down our dusty road and parked in a field close to the main house where the auction was to begin. People gathered at the window of the auctioneer's trailer, signing up for a number tag to use for bidding on items. Then they strolled over in the direction of the auctioneer as he stood talking quietly with his assistant. The assistant was holding a clipboard with a sheet of typewritten papers attached, and his job was to record the number of the item, the price and the number of the winning bidder.

Right on time, the sale began. There was a large crowd and bidding was competitive. After the household items were sold off, the auctioneer proceeded along the rows of farm equipment and accessories and then to the penned livestock themselves as the sale progressed. The house and land were to be auctioned at the end of the day to the highest bidder.

The Oleson family huddled together miserably near the house and away from the auction, silently watching as two generations of accumulated items were purchased by total strangers. Sometimes, friends of the family walked over with hugs of commiseration.

We were penned by the milking barn. I was so nervous my stomach kept churning. There was a feeling of anticipation and unease in the air. We watched as boisterous strange humans clambered out of their vehicles, slamming doors and shouting at their children as they streamed onto our farm.

I made a new friend, another Brown Swiss calf named Smokey, who was in the pen beside me. We quietly shared our fears. As we huddled close together in the fresh lined straw bed, Smokey's little body was shaking. Nerves had gotten the best of her. I, also to the point of tears, tried some words of comfort. "We'll be alright. I don't understand what's happening, but it can't get worse than the time my mother was sent away."

I looked up to see two older men stop and lean on the fence. One was seemingly upset and expressed it with deep emotion, quite loudly. "When I was on the plane coming back from my trip, two ladies seated directly behind me were talking. They were commenting on all the construction and land development."

"One lady said, 'They should develop all this land. These ignorant farmers don't need it. They are too dumb to make a living. I hate dirty, nasty cows anyway with all their flies.'

"Then she mentioned a story from her grandfather's era about the alleged practice of 'tipping cows,' which was sneaking up on a cow and pushing it over for entertainment. She said it was excused on the grounds that the cows were too stupid to know what happened.

"The two women started giggling uncontrollably until tears rolled down their cheeks. Then the other lady derisively commented, 'Factory farms are working in Europe. Why not in the United States? That farm down there (pointing out the jet's window) would make a lovely golf course!'"

He leaned on the fence grumbling, "I am so angry at myself for just listening and not speaking my mind to those old broads! Old McDonald's farm will be a thing of the past with ignorant attitudes like that. Development is devouring farmland. Farmers can't make a living raising essential food to feed Americans and we have people starving in this country. It is such a sad state."

His companion shook his head, "Why do you think this poor devil is selling out? This was a nice place once. I imagine it must be pretty hard to leave."

The other man agreed, spat a stream of tobacco juice onto the grass and said, "Yeah, we'd better go on back over to the auction and see what we can buy."

For the livestock auction, the animals were channeled into a pen next to a circular ring surrounded by people. Each animal was moved into the area and sold separately. I defecated nervously as my turn approached. Smokey went first. She charged frantically into the round enclosure and never stopped running in circles until the yelling and noise ceased, and a gate opened. She appeared as wild as a dangerous mad dog. Her price was low. People were afraid to deal with an animal having such a temperament. A gangly young bearded man bought her. He said he'd show her what "tough" meant, to nervous giggles in the crowd.

I felt proud and poised as I entered the ring. That was a momentary state, as I looked up to see humans staring and shouting. My knees shook, but I kept my head held high. Standing close to the front of the enclosure stood a slender young girl with blue eyes and braids dressed in jeans and a checkered shirt.

She nudged the lanky man dressed in bib overalls next to her. "That's her. I want her, Daddy, for my 4-H project! I'll pay for her from my savings. Isn't she beautiful?" The auctioneer was yelling garbled words into a the short stick he held up to his mouth. Two men circling the inside of the ring with me yelled, "Yea!" and pointed at a human when they raised a hand in the crowd signifying a bid. This startled me and I jumped as several people raised their hands with their numbers. I nervously paced the enclosure, peering into the crowd with large frightened brown eyes. One of the men poked me sharply with his long stick to keep me moving in the pen.

Cries of "Yup!" mingled with the man sing songing into the stick, "Whatareyagonnagive, whatareyagonnagivehere! Youngheifercowcominayearling. Gotahunertnowagimmetwo, yeahnowgimmethreehunert; goodnowfour,four,four. 'Notherhunert,doIhearfour." The human stopped abruptly and swiveled his head around the room. Silence followed him. He plaintively sang out, "Are you going to let this beautiful heifer sell at market price? Look at this refinement. Boys, you are missing a good one!" Then the shouting and sing songing began anew, and several hands went up which were quickly acknowledged by the ring men and the auctioneer.

Finally, I heard, "Going once, going twice, SOLD for fivehunertdollars to the little lady beaming from ear to ear!" A gate opened and I retreated to a pen thinking that maybe things couldn't get worse. I needed a drink, but after that ordeal I could not eat or drink. I wanted to lie down but thought it safer to stand. Being ready for whatever was next, my eyes bulging with fear and my sides heaving hard, I squeezed into the back corner, facing the gate. I could hear the next animal being herded into the ring and the frenetic shouting began again.

Fortunately for everyone concerned the rain held off but the sky remained overcast and gloomy. As the sale continued several sporadic openings in the clouds allowed shafts of sunlight to warm the people. Humans looked up smiling, grateful for even the slightest temperature increase.

A portable concession stand fed the buyers' appetites all day until almost dusk. Freshly brewed coffee permeated the air. Chili, hamburgers, brats, and sloppy joes were served until the last one was purchased.

As the final item was declared "SOLD," humans patiently queued up to the cashier's window to pay for their bargains before loading up the newest possessions. Someone was overheard saying, "Oh, I know I paid too much, but the Olesons farmed for over forty years, yet still couldn't make it. The family deserves a break." It was a good sale. No--it was a great sale as everything including the buildings and acreage was sold. The farmer and his family sorrowfully watched as their possessions were removed and hauled away.

Neighbors and strangers stopped to wish them well. Tears flowed among family and friends. The success of the auction did not alleviate the painful sadness of watching their lives' accumulations loaded up by the new owners and going down the dusty road leading from their farm. It did no good to bitterly deny their failure and blame it on the economy. Trying to be positive by repeating to themselves that this was a passage to a better future for the family was mere dust in the wind. Nothing made it easy. The pain and sorrow cut deep.

I watched as humans loaded their purchases and drove down the dirt road, clouds of dust filling the air. The barnyard became more empty and quieter than I had ever seen it. I shivered in fear, wondering what would happen next in my life.

Chapter 7

A BETTER LIFE

My friend Smokey was the first to be picked up. An old multi-colored, tarnished Ford pickup backed up to the chute. Smokey was pushed onto the ramp, slapped on the rump, and forced into the truck bed beside a mound of rusty bargains accumulated throughout the day. None of us could say "Good-bye." All of this was so strange. One after another my farm animal friends disappeared into the gaping entrances of one trailer after another, followed by the harsh slamming of the gate behind them.

I was finally loaded up just before dark. I boldly jumped into the trailer mainly out of fear, thinking, "What now?" The drive to my new home was short. I had never been in a trailer and wondered if my experience was similar to my mother's. It was not unpleasant and only slightly stressful with a low whining sound and rocking motion as I once again passed from one life to another.

The shock came after I arrived at my new home. The trailer door opened slowly as a young girl coaxed me to come out. As I displayed apprehension, she walked in beside me talking softly, gently telling me it would be all right. I bolted through the opened doorway and found myself in a tightly closed corral system.

"Daddy, can we please let her rest tonight? I'll start working with her tomorrow," she suggested. Her father nodded agreeably.

After an hour of quiet and being left to my own devices, I started walking the fence perimeter sniffing cautiously. I discovered clean cool water and my favorite grain mixture, along with sweet fragrant hay.

I thought, "Oh, this is grand," savoring every bite. After finishing what I considered dessert I became very sleepy. I lay down and immediately fell into a deep slumber.

Through a thick mist, in my exhausted mind, I felt as though some strange being was kicking me and screaming for me to get away from the food.

"You stupid animal get away!" someone else yelled over and over. "Sold. Sold. Sold" echoed through my mind. My eyes flickered. My tongue was hanging from my mouth with a tiny droplet of saliva clinging, ready to fall. My eyes fluttered open to find it was only a bad dream. The memories left me quivering as I remembered the sale. I could only guess what morning would bring, and I slept fitfully the remainder of the night.

My new owner was a cheerful girl named Heather. Her mother had died many years before, and she lived as an only child on the farm with her father. As she placed a bucket with grain and hay in the feed bunk in my pen, she perched on the fence rail above me and explained that she belonged to 4-H, an organization that encouraged members to raise, exhibit and show animals. The first competition was the county fair. Winners from that competed at the state fair level. She said it was every young 4-Hmember's dream to show and win with their animals at the State Fair. She was going to train me, she said, so I could be shown at the county fair. I had much to learn, she commented, smiling at me. Although I didn't understand what she was telling me, I loved the soft sound of her voice and it soothed my fears.

Heather was patient and loved cattle. That made all the difference. Although my mother's words "Never trust the humans" kept creeping into my mind, the kindness with which Heather treated me softened my feelings towards humans. Each day I waited to see Heather and always greeted her with a softly murmured moo. We were developing a deep bond of friendship. The human and animal association was deeply gratifying to both of us.

One day in the barn I heard her father warn, "Heather, are you spoiling that cow? She is getting pretty fat." With a twinkle in his eye he said, "You don't expect her to win at the county fair, I hope." Heather just grinned at her father and shrugged nonchalantly.

I had never seen happy humans. It took me an exceptionally long time to get past the fear of being kicked or spit upon. I responded well to kindness and was eager to please within this new association. It was surprising how much and how quickly I could learn when I wasn't afraid.

Heather approached me each day with something new. One day it was a brush and a currycomb. Brushings were pleasing, although the currycomb scratched and pulled hairs out of my tail. The next day it was a rope halter. I was shocked and reacted by pulling away when the halter was placed over my head and fastened securely with Heather's gentle hands.

"Don't take away my freedom!" I mooed as I pulled and tugged trying to get away wondering if this was the reason Mother had warned me not to trust humans. As hard as Heather pulled forward, I pulled harder in the opposite direction. She coaxed me up to a secure post and fastened the rope tightly. Stepping away from me she soothingly spoke to me and watched carefully when I realized I couldn't walk away. I braced all four legs and attempted to pull backward. The rope creaked but resisted loosening, even with all my strength. As the sweating-tired girl brushed over my neck, back and legs I pulled even harder.

"Just let me loose," I bawled angrily. "This is not fun!"

So our training went. Each day she would rub my head and ears as she clipped the lead rope onto the halter. Then she would work on teaching me to lead with her. Standing off to one side from where I stood with my feet firmly planted on the ground, she would pull steadily on the rope with her gloved hands and coax me forward. As this put me off balance, I was forced to take one stilted step after another or fall over. Grunting with the effort, she pulled, and I staggered around the pen, having no other choice. Then she would stop at the post and tie me up. Sweating and tired, she would talk softly to me as she patiently brushed my coat. My reward was being fed a ration of grain after we had completed our daily lesson.

One afternoon I decided I had resisted long enough. It was tiring and frustrating. The game was getting old. As Heather carefully lowered the halter over my head I did not resist. She looked pleasantly surprised. She backed up with only a minor expectation of me walking forward, and bracing her body to initiate the tug-of-war... and I stepped forward. Heather was startled but appeared pleasantly surprised and hugged me before leading me around the pen. From that moment on, I led like a champion.

Next, I was introduced to a long metal stick with a small hook on the end, which Heather used to stroke my belly from back-to-front. It calmed me. She used this when teaching me to walk forward, stop and place my feet on the ground so I was showing my best conformation. I was taught to pose or "set-up," back-up, hold my top line straight and stand without moving. I was never hit with this stick, only gently pushed, and prodded into position and I began to relax more with every lesson.

Another new experience was getting bathed. She tied me firmly to the post and brought out a foaming bucket filled with sudsy warm water and brushes Then (horrors!) a long, slithery thing that shot water out of the end which I thought was a snake. That terrified me. She squirted me from a safe distance starting with my legs, until I was sure the thing would not hurt.

"Silly calf," she admonished, laughing. "It's only a hose. You'll get used to it. Doesn't that feel nice and cool in the hot summer sun?"

And it did indeed. After shampooing and rinsing, she scraped the excess water off my glistening coat with a flat metal tool and then brushed my hair coat backwards.

Another day she brought out a small machine with a long hose attached to it. A high-pitched whine split the air when she touched a button and warm air blew out the end of the hose, which scared me until I understood that this wouldn't hurt me either. The blowing air quickly dried my coat while she "back brushed" the hair, making it stand up on end, giving my body a fuller appearance. This became a daily ritual and I grew to enjoy it.

The time for the fair quickly approached and the day finally came when I was once again put in the trailer and hauled to the fairgrounds. As Heather carefully unloaded me from the trailer after arriving, the veterinarian gave me some pokes and prods, listened to my heart and lungs, looked at my eyes, mouth and coat and gave me a clean Bill of Health.

Then Heather led me into the cattle barn and tied me securely in a roomy stall which was knee deep in soft, fragrant straw. It was the softest bedding I had ever slept in. It was so deep, that none of my body parts touched the hard, cold cement underneath. There were huge fans whirling noisily overhead to keep the barn cool. Actually, they were somewhat annoying because of the noise, but I got used to that, too. Heather then brought in a bucket of water and tied it to the fence so I wouldn't knock it over, then placed a bucket of grain and hay on the ground for me to eat.

Her father had painstakingly built and varnished a sturdy wooden show box on wheels to keep the grooming supplies she needed. It contained brushes, halters, a blanket and special bucket with my name on them, along with bottles and cans of products to make me look my best. This was placed beside my stall for easy access. I looked around cautiously before starting in on the grain and hay. So much food and fresh water. Bovines love to eat, and this was a smorgasbord. Food aplenty. I lay and ate. I stood and ate. When I awakened from naps, I ate some more. This must be heaven.

There was an overwhelming atmosphere of excitement looming over the fairgrounds. It appeared to envelop everyone who entered the gates, especially the animals. A cacophony of noise surrounded the fairgrounds as all types of animals arrived and were penned or stalled according to their type. It looked, felt and smelled like a large barnyard with humans milling about getting their animals settled in their new quarters.

I was brushed and bathed regularly. Heather loved to squirt me with water during the rinsing part of my bath. If I got water in my ears it tickled, and I would shake my head violently from side to side. Heather laughed. Such a spectacle! Wet girl, wet cow!

In the stall on my right stood a very large cow named Lucy. She was elegant and carried herself accordingly. However, Lucy had a strange habit that did not fit with her typically graceful motions. Each morning her human left a bucket of clean water for Lucy to drink. She would sniff, raise her upper lip and carefully placed her front feet and legs in the center of the bucket. She gave a soft sigh and stood chewing her cud as her feet soaked in the cool water. It was an unusual sight.

Sometimes humans walking by stopped to look. Most of them laughed and pointed. I'm not sure why, because most of them had no idea what normal cow behavior included, but I had never seen a cow do this and it was amusing to watch. Of course, happy humans provide great comfort to their animals and we loved that.

At the fairgrounds, the young 4-Hers exercised their animals by haltering them and leading them around. I was spooked at first, looking at all the new strange things and listening to crowds of boisterous people, but Heather stroked my coat and talked to me and I trusted and followed her without causing any problems. Other animals did the same up and down the rows, around the dirt arena of the grandstand area. Then it was back to my stall, to be tied up and fed again.

One early morning, however, Heather came to my stall and abruptly untied me, prodding me saying, "Get up, Marla, it's showtime." Heather was acting very strangely.

This made me nervous and I balked, pulling and bellowing before walking beside her to the wash station. Grabbing a bucket of water, with the brushes and rags she quickly cleaned me up so I would look my best. A new brown leather halter was placed over my head with a leather lead line. My tail was combed, ratted up and sprayed, giving it the appearance of a stiff ball swinging side to side like a pendulum as I walked.

No one took time for breakfast this morning as getting ready for the show was too important. Everyone was too anxious.

Heather tied me in my stall, then vanished for a few minutes, returning later in a long-sleeved white blouse, new blue jeans and polished boots. Her hair had been pulled back from her face and was held in place by a blue ribbon.

She untied me and began leading me toward the big arena to wait in line for our show class. As I followed her quietly, I noticed that she had a white piece of paper with a black number pinned to her back.

When we got there, it was chaos, with some of the cattle running frantically around their owners, who grasped the lead line trying to get control. More out of fear and trust, I stayed next to Heather.

We stood in line for 35 minutes waiting for our turn in the arena. Many of the animals attempted to lie down. Young impatient exhibitors tugged to keep them moving. Cows can be stubborn and more often than not it took the humans many hard pulls and a firm voice to manage their obstinate, powerful cattle. One young girl started crying in frustration.

A tall boy kicked his animal each time it attempted to lie down. The tension in the air was palpable.

Finally, the large gate swung open and we walked briskly into an arena with people all around. Heather whispered, "This is it, girl. Please be good. Make us proud!" She gently rubbed under my chin, set me up and stroked my belly with the metal stick. Then I lifted my head and followed Heather's lead. What else was there to do? I trusted this girl.

After being led around the ring several times we were motioned to stop, back up and set up to pose. Then the show judge, a heavyset man who was highly regarded by the exhibitors walked around each of us, peering closely and sometimes touching and poking an animal. After he had selected the best of us, a loud voice announced the names and numbers of the winners. Heather's mouth dropped and she tried to hold back a grin as she whispered, "We won! We got first place!" The ring steward handed her a blue ribbon as we exited the arena. Heather wept, threw her arms around my neck and kissed me. "Thank you, girl. Oh, how I love you! This means we're going to the State Fair!"

Later, pictures of Heather and me were taken by a professional photographer hired by the Fair Board as a remembrance of our fair experience. Her proud father hugged his daughter and people laughed and shook hands with them as Heather led me back to my stall for a good feeding and brushing.

Too soon the fair ended, and we were busy loading up and heading home to prepare for the for the next exhibition. The question on Heather's mind was, could we win at the State Fair?

CHAPTER 8

MINNESOTA STATE FAIR

For the next month, Heather and I were inseparable. She started sleeping in the barn stall with me. I couldn't believe it, right next to me, often touching me with her head lying on my shoulders. We practiced leading, backing and posing. I was brushed hundreds of strokes each day and then blanketed to add that special glow. I was so happy just to be at home.

Late one evening, while I was dozing off to sleep, Heather told me that the Minnesota State Fair was highly competitive. This was much, much bigger than the county fair including the confusion and noise.

Almost before I knew it, Heather and her father were loading up the trailer with feed, grooming supplies and everything else she would need for the Minnesota State Fair. Once I was secure in the trailer, we headed out. Everything at this fair appeared much larger and more hurried.

Although I had been at the County Fair and felt comfortable, many more people and animals bustled around the larger fairgrounds. The air was thick with the feeling of Hurry! Hurry! Heather and her father appeared very tired by the time they were through with the vet check, hauling supplies to my show stall, and getting settled. I had never seen this much activity and was extremely nervous about being in such unfamiliar surroundings.

The sounds of cattle bellowing, sheep and goats bleating, hogs squealing and roosters crowing at all hours of the day put me off my feed and I ignored the sweet grain, fragrant hay and fresh water in front of me. All I could do was look around at all the bustle. It was not until after sunset that things quieted down enough for me to relax enough to eat. I slept fitfully in my bed, though I was exhausted.

Heather came early the next morning and took me to the wash rack for a shampoo, blow-dry and loving before she took me back to the stall for breakfast. She talked with me as I ate, and the soothing sound of her voice was so calming. Later that morning, she haltered me and walked around the grounds for exercise and to gain familiarity with the grounds. The rest of the day was spent relaxing and preparing for the cattle show the next day.

The day of the show was hectic and began with a trip to the wash rack as Heather bathed, brushed and dried my glossy coat. Then she sprayed and back-combed my coat and tail until she was satisfied I looked my best, although preening never stopped. Putting on the leather show halter, she led me out of the stall toward the expansive arena, where a large number of cattle waited with their hopeful owners.

Show time came quickly but instead of waiting for 35 minutes, we waited in various lines for nearly two hours. It was hot with very little breeze and exhibitors and animals moved impatiently.

As we waited, we noticed one small cow two classes before mine that kept scratching and attempting to rub against any object, including the young girl holding the halter. This poor cow had large bald spots and flaking skin. The veterinarian was called over to inspect her. With a look of disgust, he noted verbally that she had blood-sucking lice. They itched unbearably and caused great discomfort. The handler and the animal were immediately asked to leave. The red-faced young exhibitor hurriedly led the cow away from the crowd and straight to the trailer to be loaded up so as not to infect any other cattle.

How could this have happened?

Somehow, this animal's registration for the fair had never contained a proper health certificate. The owner hoped by blanketing her they could sneak into the show and the overworked veterinarian hadn't looked underneath the blanket at the animal's coat. It had nearly worked. Although I felt sorry for the poor cow, my skin itched for several days and Heather treated me for lice after the fair just in case I had become infected.

Finally, our class was called, and once we entered the huge dome-shaped arena it was similar to the county fair experience. Heather kept a tight grip on the halter. She appeared incredibly nervous. Judges used the same criteria as the smaller fairs only much more intense. Spectators cheered as the winners were announced in each class. This time, Heather did not jump with excitement as no one handed us a ribbon. Exiting the ring, the judge commented, "A very fine heifer. I might have placed her higher in the group if she had not been over-conditioned." As Heather led me slowly back to my stall, her father gently suggested, "Ahhh, maybe she should have had more exercise and not so much of that beloved grain?"

Heather glumly agreed but hugged me, nevertheless. Although I did not win, we were both proud of our efforts and there was nothing to be ashamed of. There was always next year. Later that evening while unwinding from the stress of the show, Heather and her friends sat together on her show box discussing the seminar they had attended that evening.

A guest lecturer from Colorado State University, Dr. Bernard Rollin, was an animal ethicist and considered an expert on animal welfare. He told the audience that animals have rights just like people, and Heather's friends agreed. He defined these rights as, "essentially the right to spend their lives in an environment that suits their biological nature and minimizes physical and psychological stress or suffering."

He continued, stating that historically going as far back as the ancient Greeks and Romans, nearly all the people were involved with agriculture. There was an appreciation for the land. It had to be preserved and protected. People knew the connection between their food source and survival. They understood that caring for the land and animals meant survival.

Now only 1.3% of the population is actually involved with farming, ranching or food production. The connection to the land is missing. We have an additional problem in that our rural society has improved production to such an extent that there is typically a surplus of foodstuffs. Not only does this keep prices low, but as consumers go to the abundantly increasing numbers of outlets, food is so plentiful it is taken for granted. No wonder they forget the farmers and ranchers. An understanding and appreciation for how food is produced is essential for both groups. Dr. Rollin went on to say that good animal husbandry could improve with just a few basic changes. These include:

- Use anesthesia for castrations (or raise bulls) and for dehorning
- Adopt alternative identification methods in place of hot branding
- Emphasize humane handling practices when training new employees
- Update processing equipment to reduce stress in slaughterhouses
- Improve barns and facilities to provide a comfortable living environment, including shade, windbreaks, and good drainage

In summary Dr. Rollin noted that 'rough treatment of the animal causes bruising of the meat and costs the industry $22 million annually as bruised meat cannot be used. He stated there was definitely room for improvement." (Remember, this was in the 60's!) The crowd left with a better understanding of livestock production in a humane and ethical manner, and the hum of excited conversation followed the attendees out the door.

The last day of the fair was quiet. The pursuit of excellence was over and the tired bodies sagged, both the humans and us critters. We all needed to rest. Heather had enough energy remaining to attend a poster board exhibition in the main hall. This was a judged competition and typically interesting enough to attract many people. One of the better displays was a poster regarding the nine behavioral traits displayed by cattle. Although the classifications were too difficult to remember, the types of behaviors were not.

Heather excitedly told her friends she had witnessed almost all of these just by observing the herd. The first was fighting which was more predominant in males than females. The second type was mimicking as when one cow got up and walked toward the barn the others proceeded to follow. All of the teenagers listening agreed they had observed the next behavior which was the caregiving or maternal type. This was one of their favorites as bovine mothers often conversed with their children in a loving, kind manner. One of the teens said he wished his parents talked as kindly to him and his sisters. Heather did not let this interruption stop her enjoyment and learning. She had taken careful notes and referred to them as she spoke. "We have all watched cows go to the bathroom. As silly as it sounds this is referred to as the elimination behavior." Everyone laughed.

"If you think that's funny, the section on sexual behaviors went into explicit detail," she commented, her face reddening. After that, several of the young men grinned at each other, then got up and said they were going to visit the display and see for themselves.

Once again Heather continued, turning the page to her notes. "As cows do typically wander in groups this action is called gregarious behavior. The action of eating, grazing, and suckling is touted as the ingestive behavior."

Her last notes detailed the investigative behavior of a cow. Everyone listening knew cows were the most curious creatures in the world. I listened for the next hour as different young humans told their stories of troublesome and inquisitive cows.

Heather and her friends contemplated these new terms and pondered the ways in which it could help them if they chose to carry on the farm traditions. Most of these young teens had watched their parents struggle and never have adequate money to pay for the necessities. Why would they want to continue that kind of lifestyle? The saying that "it gets in your blood," spoke to the determination they were raised with. Even though they worked hard, life was often unrewarding financially, However, they would always miss the animals if they left and this was the understanding; it was ingrained in their hearts and souls.

The stress of this event had left me tired. I was ready to go home and just be a normal cow on the farm. My skin was becoming sensitive to baths and combs. The detergents left my skin dry and I started itching all over again. Heather used conditioning oil after my last show bath rubbing it into my coat carefully.

Chapter 9

FARM LIFE

When the entourage arrived back home, I was put out to pasture with the other young heifers my age. One morning, I watched as Heather walked to the end of the driveway and waited until a large square box on wheels stopped and the door opened. It looked like she was eaten. She disappeared inside, the door closed, and the monster rumbled down the dirt road, dust blowing in its wake.

I missed Heather deeply. I did not walk far out to the pasture with the others. I took a position closest to where Heather vanished into the jaws of the beast. It was not easy waiting, but I stood patiently feeling in my heart that my friend would return. That first day was the hardest, but late in the afternoon the contraption returned, and she stepped out and onto the ground, smiling and waving to someone inside.

I mooed and cried as I saw her running towards me. I was so happy to see her! Heather threw her arms around my neck murmuring, "I missed you so much. I thought about you all day."

Later that evening she visited by the pasture gate, explaining, "That big ol' machine is a school bus. I'm going to be gone during the day, but I'll come to visit you when I get home. School's back in session, and I can't wait to tell my friends all about my summer." Heather unlatched the gate and slipped through it, spending precious time brushing and talking to me. I thoroughly enjoyed the attention. Just before dark as Heather was called to dinner, and the other girls watched with envy as Heather kissed me goodnight.

This routine went on for nearly a week before I gave up watching her leave and return. Eventually I watched for the big orange bus from the lush meadow, now content to be with my bovine friends.

Slowly she and I went about our own lives still beaming with joy every time our paths crossed. I liked trusting a human. I liked having Heather for a best friend. I also started forming deeper bonds within my herd.

There was Bird, so named because of the solid black coloring of a blackbird. Bird was extremely free spirited. She was the boss, and everyone knew not to test her resolve. As Judge Judy is known as the judge with the attitude, Bird was the cow with the attitude. Beware the wrath of either. It was not pleasant. It was fortunate for this independent spirit that her humans appreciated both her beauty and the show quality breeding potential.

Another cow named Bessie was quite timid. She had been abused by a previous owner so badly that there was no coming back for her. She ate by herself usually some distance from the group or waited to eat until the others were finished before coming to the feed trough. If humans approached for any reason Bessie looked up, fear flashing in her eyes and would gallop to the far end of the pasture. She would stand there watching fretfully until they left.

One time two humans cornered Bessie in the pasture to throw a lariat over her neck. The cow panicked and bolted breaking through five strands of barbed wire fence at the end of the pasture before she was caught. Deep cuts oozed with blood over her brisket and front legs. After being coaxed back through the break and along the fence line to the barn she had to be put in the squeeze chute for everyone's safety to be doctored. She was very stiff and sore and limped for days. Both the internal and external healing was slow.

We had a real peacemaker in our group, a sweet, quiet, lovely-dispositioned cow named Kathleen. Everyone loved Kathleen including the humans. They loved to pet her and scratch under her neck. We loved her because she listened and cared. I told her about my mother and the way she disappeared. She consoled me by saying how lucky I was to have run free for so long. Kathleen made everyone in the barnyard feel special just by listening. She was kind, gentle and had an easygoing manner.

We also had bullies in the herd. It didn't matter how far away from them you grazed, out of the corner of your eye you'd see them charging over to start a ruckus. Usually the submissive animal just moved out of the way and let the ornery cows have what they wanted, often a tasty bunch of clover. We learned quickly that it wasn't worth a fight or a bruise.

We grew taller that summer and filled out more as our bodies matured. It was restful and peaceful. Grasses grew so statuesque we could eat chest high munching away hours each day. Birds chirped and sang gaily, never leaving our side and hopping alongside us as we grazed. At times they perched on our backs eating the bugs that lived in our coats that our tails couldn't swat off. Others would stop by for a quick meal of the grains shed by the grasses and "wave" to us with their wings as they flew back into the big open sky.

One morning a truck and trailer pulled up to the gate. Heather and her father stepped out of the noisy vehicle, opened the back end of the trailer and stood there motionless. Nothing happened for a brief period of time. All of us turned our heads expectantly, eyes fixed, waiting. What was it? We heard something move in the trailer. It was large enough to scrape the walls as it moved.

No-Fear-Kathleen took a step closer nose twitching, waiting. As she did, a young bull stepped up to the opening looking quizzically at each of us. He was quite handsome. He gingerly stepped down onto the soil losing some of his tremendous stature. Bird walked over to him, put her head to his and bunted, challenging his undeclared authority. He appeared startled but braced all four legs to hold his position. Bird backed up and rushed, clashing head to head again. Again, she charged, this time striking his shoulder. He turned quickly and spun around, his tail swishing furiously. He put his head down, snorted and stoutly approached Bird straight on. He pushed her backwards at a run for several steps. Now Bird looked startled but only paused momentarily while she regrouped to ram him again.

As the full impact of her force struck his neck, he went down on one knee. Immediately back up, he squared off, attempting to catch Bird off guard and force her backwards. But this time she was prepared and dug in all four feet braced. Since he outweighed her, there was little competition even with Bird's confidence. He moved her backwards, then stood still in a silent challenge, daring her to try again. Poor Bird suffered a major defeat in front of her friends. Her ego was bruised. She turned, tossed her head in the air with indignation and moved away, bucking and kicking. The rest of us, serving as silent spectators, walked over to meet the victor. The humans smiled, climbed into the front of the truck and drove back up the road in a cloud of dust.

Our new companion's name was Abe. He was a young bull brought to court us young female cows. That meant nothing to us until things began changing one climactic morning. Each of us woke up in an unusual mood, looking at Abe with a twinkle in our eye. He eyed us all, then picked one that was eyeing him, strutted over licking and gently nudging her neck. He enticed the heifer to walk off with him and they spent the day playfully frolicking. In the evening they bedded together away from the group. The pair ate side by side, nuzzling more frantically with each passing hour. Gently, Abe mounted the now docile cow until there was a surge of pressure released. Abe, sides heaving, groaned a huge sigh of relief as he stood back on the ground. He stayed with his female companion for another day, being ever so attentive and following the same ritual with the next cow. Then he would move off to graze complacently away from the others, while the newly bred bovine rejoined the herd. Something was different about that cow, a new sense of purpose.

I had been very nonchalant towards Abe. He seemed nice enough, but I had other friends. Besides, a cow's commanding urge is to eat. We spend 16 hours a day consuming everything in sight. There isn't much time to pay attention to an outsider who stays off by himself. Then one morning I awoke with a stranger feeling than I had ever known. It was intense. It was stronger than the desire to forage. Now I became curious about where Abe was grazing. It turned out Abe was also curious about me and shuffled in my direction. Soon he was standing close to me with an amorous look on his face.

He sniffed and licked various places on my coat moving around me until he reached my tail. Sniffing my vulva, he raised his head. The first third of his nose was wrinkled and his lip was curled upwards exposing all his teeth. He mooed quietly inviting me to follow him. We ambled away from the others touching bodies ever so slightly.

Something wild seemed about to explode inside each of us. He was so gentle, so knowing yet with a glint in his eye. He licked my neck with his tongue. I quivered. It felt so natural. I had never experienced any urge stronger than eating until now.

Abe walked behind me again, smelled me and raised his nostrils to the wind. He uttered a low moo that increased in intensity. He tried to mount me from behind, but I was startled and moved away. I was skittish yet I enjoyed the foreplay. Getting more serious now was not linked to my biological clock.

I sauntered back in front to peer into Abe's eyes. There was fire, a burning urge that calmed with gentle anticipation. He walked beside me, touching. He nosed my thigh, then rising on his powerful back legs, placed his front legs gently on either side of my hips. He stood there for only seconds, immobilized, and then thrusting forward. It felt right, but I walked edgily out from under him again. This time I continued walking, but only six or seven steps, as Abe trotted directly in front, blocking my passage.

He moved and stood farther away from the others for more privacy, hoping it would help my mood. We continued this game all day, frolicking until sunset. Each time I moved to avoid penetration, but each time letting him get just a little closer. I noticed a deepening urge telling me to let it go in. Abe was still desirous, frantically so, yet patiently waiting. He came up, licked my face several times, and stood motionless. Then he walked around to my rump, and licked my swollen, juicy vulva. I moved my tail to one side. After another gentle lick, he reared up, his sides heaving breathlessly. He was poised almost weightlessly over my back, supporting his massive structure on his springing back legs. His two front legs straddled my back holding on with a powerful force. Something warm and pulsing was up inside my body. Such a force was beyond my control. I let it happen. I enjoyed.

We slept side by side that night with soft moos passing between us. Early the next morning before the sun was up, Abe got up without even a backward glance and walked away to the far side of the field, contentedly grazing once again. I noticed Abe spent time with each of us ladies over the next couple of months, until all of my friends had been bred by Abe and new life was growing inside us.

Within a couple of weeks, I noticed something different happening to my body. I felt calmer, more relaxed. I didn't feel the need to head bunt or race with my friends. I wandered off to be by myself. If a cow can develop a more voracious appetite, that was my fate. It seemed as if I was always hungry. Grazing became an obsession.

Then one day Heather's father appeared and herded Abe in a determined manner along the fence line toward the barnyard. He had served his purpose. Abe left reluctantly, climbing back into the trailer, displaying his unhappiness by flipping his tail. We had become his family and he hated to be separated from us.

Winter came and left quite unremarkably. This year was mild. There was plenty of feed and water. The whole herd was content and happy, as were the humans. I was getting accustomed to friendly, happy humans, good food and creature comforts I had not known before. I was also getting accustomed to becoming larger with each passing day, especially my stomach and expanding girth. My walk slowed, and Heather frequently stopped by to see how I was doing. She had a job in town now, so we spent less time together. I missed her, but something else more important was happening in my life.

Each day, morning and early evening now, the hired man came to the pasture and yelled, "Come cows, come girls." One by one the elder cows would rise and walk the lane in the direction of the milking barn. I learned to follow along, then turned and went into my own stall. We tried to do this quickly because each of us was given grain. As we ate, we were quietly chained into place. The tasty feed was worth the walk.

Hmmm. I didn't know why we went through this ritual, but it was rewarding. Once I was secured in my stanchion, Heather or the hired man would rub my udder and pet my flanks, talking soothingly. I soon became accustomed to this and was not afraid of being confined. Once the lactating cows had been milked, we were all released and followed one another back out to the pasture for the evening.

The growth in my abdomen continued to increase at an alarming rate. It was hard to walk. My vulva was so swollen and sore that it hurt constantly. I could feel strong movement within me, and I fretted about this, wondering what would happen next. One night I was sorted from the others and taken through a gate into a pen knee-deep in straw in the well-lit barn.

Chapter 10

THE CALVING

A little while later, Heather came into the pen beside me with her father. "Do you think it's tonight? Will she calve tonight? She is late. I was hoping she would have a little heifer, but late ones are usually bulls."

Her father replied, "If she doesn't go tonight we should probably call the vet and have him check to see if everything is all right."

I only knew that I was the focus of attention, so I went into a corner to lie down, chewing my cud contently as they quietly left.

It was around midnight when my labor started. I stood up and defecated nervously. I attempted to urinate but was powerless to push. With increasing intensity, the pains continued for several hours. I stood up and lay back down many times as time passed. I switched my tail with a furor, hoping it would help, but to no avail. Either Heather or her father came to check on me regularly, reporting no change yet.

Then at 4:00 a.m., Heather's father came to check again. "Well, dear lady," he soothed. "This is it. You're going to be a mother."

He left momentarily to awaken Heather and bring a bucket of warm water. As he rolled up his sleeves, Heather squirted Betadine disinfectant into the bucket. I was lying in the soft straw, weary from having been up and down so many times since the contractions initiated. I got up as Heather came to my head, and her father walked to my tail, which he lifted gently. "Hold her and talk to her so she isn't scared. This will hurt."

As he started inserting his hand between the swollen lips of my vulva, I stood up again, switching my tail back and forth. I shifted my weight anxiously from foot to foot. My front feet pawed the ground, striking when the pain intensified. He inserted his bare arm up to his elbow, feeling, probing. "Aauugh," he growled, "The calf is backwards. We are going to have to turn it around or it won't survive."

I was experiencing a heightened sense of awareness and sensitivity. Everything was hurting. Heather's father proceeded to blindly follow the body contours floating inside me with his strong arm. Heather, trying to stay calm, whispered into my ear. "It will be all right. Just hang on."

Sweat poured down her father's face. The muscles in his arms and chest bulged. "This is a tough one. It's so big. I'm having trouble getting the head and front feet positioned properly". He grunted and stood on his toes to lengthen his reach. "I'm not sure I'm strong enough. There! I found a front leg." Grabbing hold, he felt for the head. It was straight back, so it had to be shifted forward. Slowly and painfully, using every ounce of reserve strength, the man pulled the calf around to position it properly for birth. As he removed his arm from inside me, he fell to his knees.

"Are you all right, Dad?" Heather asked anxiously.

"Sure. I just need a minute," he sighed. "That was the hardest part."

"Is the calf alive? Heather asked hesitantly.

"Yes, it seemed fine, fighting me all the way," he grinned. "Now let's sit back and let Marla do the rest." Within seconds I had to lie down again, and I began to heave and push forcefully downward. I had never experienced such distress. Nothing to do but instinctively bear down. The contractions were laborious and excruciating. They ceased momentarily and I sighed with relief, but not for long. Another sharp prolonged pain, only more intense. The timing between them shortened and the pain increased as my body rhythmically moved to force the new calf into the world.

"Look, there are the feet and nose," Heather whispered excitedly. I pushed again forcefully with every ounce of strength being depleted from my muscles. Heather grabbed the front feet and ever so gently pulled in unison with the contraction. The head and neck protruded; now the front shoulders were being expelled. As the front shoulders came through the swollen, torn opening, the remainder of the wet flaccid body poured onto the ground.

The calf was suspended in a torn sac of amniotic fluid. The umbilical cord had broken loose. The tired man cleared the gooey liquid from the nose and mouth and then tickled a nostril with a stem of hay to make the calf sneeze–and breathe. Then the seemingly lifeless form blew a wad of mucus from within its tiny nostrils and raised its neck. Shaking its small head, the frail neck only barely managed to stay upright.

With the calf now on the ground, I groaned and stood up, relieved that the birthing was over. Afterbirth hung down underneath my tail. I had seen other cows calve and knew that would soon be expelled completely. My motherly instincts and my experience with my loving mother told me this frail little creature was my responsibility. I started licking and nuzzling, my baby, my rough tongue covering the warm little body in rhythmic strokes, stimulating the calf into emitting a hoarse cry.

"Oooh, Dad, it *is* a little girl!" cried Heather. "Can we leave the calf with her, if only for today?"

"You know it will be harder on her when we move the little thing," said her father. "But it's your decision."

"Then let's leave them alone," decided Heather firmly.

After my little daughter had nourished herself on my colostrum for 24 hours, she was taken away from me and would be bottle-raised. This was very hard, and I cried for several days, but Heather had done a very caring thing. She placed my calf in the closest hutch to the fence. I was never far away and came by often just to check her.

I was now officially on the milk line, although for the first 72 hours I gave only colostrum, which was saved and fed to my calf. Three times a day I entered the milking barn, received grain, and was milked. This was painful at first because my swollen udder throbbed. The helpers were gentle though, and with each passing day the swelling subsided.

One day walking out of the barn with Pickles, who was a young cow that had not calved, I told her, "The pain was awful but once it is over you have this soft warm, tiny baby to nuzzle. Don't worry, Pickles. You'll be all right."

But Pickles was not all right. So many first-time heifers are not all right when they give birth. Pickles' udder was so swollen that getting up one morning, she stepped on a teat and tore it with her sharp hoof.

The veterinarian had to be called. The teat was hanging by a thread of skin. Grimly he offered, "We can try to sew it back on and line up the ducts, but the infection risk is high even with antibiotics. You could stall a few days to see if she'll have her calf and at least save that. It's a mess. I am very sorry." The decision was made to wait until she delivered, and the wound was cleaned thoroughly and left to drain.

Cows give milk from four quarters of their udder. If they lose the use of a quarter, their value is decreased substantially. Large efficient dairies do not contend with an animal not giving 100%. Generally, they are sold for slaughter. On rare occasions they end up at a smaller dairy or utilized as a nurse cow to raise multiple babies.

A few days later, Pickles went into prolonged labor. The veterinarian was called again, as things were not progressing. He checked Pickles and quickly noted, "We need to do a Caesarian. The calf is quite large. The cow's pelvis is too small to deliver normally. No way is she able to have that calf without surgery."

Pickles, standing upright, in great pain, was given an epidural. The pain ceased and she soon had no feeling in her back section. Her tail went limp. The vet went to her side. Using a local anesthetic, he injected her muscles at evenly spaced intervals, following the pattern of a backward seven. He allowed 15 minutes for the drug to take effect. As it did, he carefully shaved the hair on her side with electric clippers, and thoroughly cleansed the area with Betadine.

Taking out a new sterile blade for his scalpel, he inserted it, ready to make the first incision. With the glimmering blade firmly pressed to the shaved skin surface, a six-inch incision was made. Pickles stood nervously with all the attention and sensed that it was inappropriate to move. Her skin twitched. Blood ran down her side, pooling at the vet's feet. Poor Pickles just stood with eyes wide, not knowing what to expect. The surgeon continued to cut through multiple layers of tissue. He slowed, careful to stop short of cutting the stomach lining. Now to find the uterus. He laboriously pulled it closer to his original incision. He delicately cut through the uterine wall, using his finger as a guide to avoid cutting the fetus. He enlarged the incision, making room for the body to be pulled free. "I need help now," he ordered. "Grab a leg. All of us must pull together. We must go straight up and then out. Listen carefully to me so we don't rip the mother."

They pulled together in unison, but the end result was a lifeless body. Every effort to stimulate the calf to breathe proved futile. After long minutes, the vet stood up slowly saying, "I am very sorry. You might as well sell this cow. Due to her small pelvis and hip structure, she'll never be able to have a normal calf. Let's get her sewed up. I won't give her antibiotics, so she can be slaughtered right away. We'll wash the incision with Betadine."

Early the next morning, Pickles was loaded up in a trailer, hauled to the auction barn and sold. Again, I cried. It was hard seeing Pickles leave.

Fortunately, the rest of the other first year heifers calved uneventfully, and milk production went back into high gear as the new mothers' calves were pulled off and the cows made their trips through the milking barn. Our lives settled into a steady routine of good food, kindness and bountiful milk production.

Passing seasons turned into years. One day Heather no longer got on the school bus, and excitedly told me she was going to go to "college." I did not understand that, and her friends came and went as she got ready to leave, their excited, laughing voices carrying over to my pasture after milking was done. I missed having her visit me, however infrequently, and longingly remembered past memories with her.

I was bred each year and bore fine, healthy calves. I never grew used to having them taken away shortly after birth and cried each time we were separated. Then it was back to the milking parlor for another few months before I was bred again.

Time passed pleasantly enough to my way of thinking, and I learned to accept the life of a dairy cow, as I was treated well at my farm. Sadly however, I learned this was not true for every cow at every dairy.

Chapter 11

CHANGE

At the property next to my farm, I gained a new fence partner. Ruth was one of the cows in the neighbor's dairy herd. As we became acquainted, stories of her life reminded me of the old days. One day she told me what she had recently gone through in the milking barn.

"I think my human hates his life," Ruth related. "He grumbles that he's been farming his whole life and says he's becoming poorer every year. He complains about his deteriorating health. He said his wife left him and moved away with his best friend, and now he's just hanging on by a thread, hoping to keep his place. "What will that mean for us?" Ruth wondered aloud.

The neighbor's buildings were rotting from neglect and boards were loosely hanging down. The house stood, roof sagging and peeling paint dangling like shreds of cheese, showing unpainted boards beneath. Gutters had fallen off and were strewn over the yard.

Old farms did not have milking parlors. Cows were milked side by side standing in a stanchion in a barn. Directly behind them was an eight-inch cement gutter running the length of the barn, where feces and urine were shoveled for collection after milking. Each day, the farmer cleaned these shallow ditches with a shovel and wheelbarrow. It was physically demanding work.

Diana R. Wright & Rita J. Cayou

As cows lay in their muddy pens prior to milking, their tails became soaked with urine. In this swirling reeking pool, the foul-smelling liquid clung to them as they made their way to the barn.

"It isn't only me," Ruth said smugly, "But all of us have mastered subtle methods of revenge-provoking little antics."

Ruth told me that one night she was in an awful mood. As her human attached the milking machine cups to her teats, she gave a quick flip of her urine-soaked tail and slapped him directly across the face. Urine dripped from each corner of his mouth and stung his eyes. He grimaced and spat furiously, the taste of cow urine being especially repulsive and offensive, as one might imagine.

Some days Ruth's actions would have gone unpunished. Today was not that day. The poor man had been up since 4:00 a.m. He had received his inadequate milk check for last month's production, which was not enough to make his mortgage payment. Milk prices were down again, disappointingly low.

The farmer snapped. He staggered outside wiping urine from his eyes to recover his vision and reached for any object he could swing. With a deeply reddened face and glazed eyes, he started hitting Ruth with a long, rounded stick. He struck the aging cow over her ribs. Three bones gave a brisk popping sound and cracked. He raised his weapon beating her again and again until the stick broke, then tossing it aside, by now at the pinnacle of frustration, he moved behind the quivering animal and kicked so viciously and so blindly, that he only thrust into the air.

Shoving her backwards out of the milking stall, he chased her out of the barn screaming, "You fucking stupid animal. Get out of the barn before I get a gun and kill you! You're not worth a damn anyway, you old scarecrow bitch."

As Ruth told me the story, I glanced over her battered body to see the wounds layered over her skin. It was obvious Ruth would never heal on the inside and would carry scars for the rest of her life.

80

We met by the fence for another year or so. Things did not get better and then one day Ruth and her herd were loaded into a long trailer that disappeared in a cloud of dust down the dirt road. I hope they went to a human with fresh ideas and new enthusiastic attitudes. They deserved better than the life they were living.

I had my own problems, but as I aged, perceptions changed. Heather was offered a job far away from the farm. She and her father discussed it at great length under a tree in the pasture. I listened nearby, chewing quietly.

Her father was showing early signs of health problems and had been diagnosed with beginning stages of lung cancer.

"Heather, your old man is starting to show his age," he shook his head sadly. "The news from the doctor is not good and he wants me to start chemotherapy as soon as possible." Heather started crying softly and gave her father a big hug. "This is not a good time for me to leave. What should I do?"

"You must do what makes you happy and follow your dreams," he counseled. We can talk by phone and we'll get together to visit. I couldn't stand the idea of a farm sale, so I have been selling the cows here and there. There isn't much left. Once people hear you are slowing down, they start circling like vultures for a good deal. We have done well over the years, better than most. It is time to end an era. It's been a good life."

"Heather, not to change the subject, but we have some friends coming to visit from Colorado. They have a 2,000-acre ranch which they inherited from his uncle. They run a herd of mixed beef cows. This fellow comes from a long-time ranching family. His name is Jim. He has a wife named Lorrie and four children. They're a nice family. We have only spoken over the phone. I went to school with his father, who passed a few years back. They'll be here next week. Since you'll still be here you can meet them. Besides, with their four children I could use the extra help and this farm could use some excitement for a few days."

The family arrived in an old Chevy pickup truck with paint peeling off the dinged-up camper shell. The truck and tires had seen better days.

The family was so happy to have reached their destination, they all talked at once. This was their first vacation. None of them had been to Minnesota. They were hoping to do some fishing in the river. They had been told about the suckers swimming upstream. Did we really spear them? Could we eat them?

They spent the next few evenings sitting on the porch talking about ranching versus farming. It sounded to me like ranching was the same as farming; a way to raise children, but not a way to make any money. The work was hard; it had to be in your blood. When you inherit a ranch, it gets in your blood. Lorrie had to work outside of the home to provide extra income and health insurance for the family She wished the ranch could support them all, but even with small mortgage payments, the money never quite stretched.

Lorrie and the children fell in love with me at first sight. Although they had a ranch and knew nothing about milking a cow, they wanted to buy me. They convinced themselves that I would produce enough milk to provide the family with fresh nourishment and butter. They would take turns milking. Heather's father explained that milking was twice each day for 9 months of the year. He also explained that dairy cows must have grain and better-quality hay than the beef animals.

Jim was reluctant to buy a milk cow because he knew that eventually this would come down to another chore for him to oversee. He couldn't imagine a skinny old dairy cow mixing with his fat tough beef cattle. "Can she forage? Pastures get short in Colorado. We don't like to supplement feed in the winter. The cows have to graze. Sometimes they get pretty thin. She will need extra care in the winter. I can't imagine a cow like that would be able to survive a storm."

Lorrie and the children eventually won him over and promised they would love me and give me everything I needed. Everything was settled except a way to haul me to Colorado. Then Jim's oldest son suggested renting a U-Haul horse trailer. He had seen one on the lot as they passed through town.

I was a bit longer than the people who designed the two-wheeled trailer had imagined. They took out the center partition and I stood diagonally in the trailer with my tail hanging over the half door. The good news about standing diagonally was that I could not shift my weight in the trailer. Shifting weight caused the truck to weave, especially an old, under-powered truck that was already overloaded. The other good news was that I was dried up and scheduled to calve in 45-60 days. I did not have to be milked on the way home. All four children moaned at that disappointing news.

The drive from Minnesota to Colorado was long and hot. The old truck had to be coaxed along and the tires just wouldn't cooperate. Two blowouts, both on the freeway, caused unusual delays. Jim and Lorrie took turns driving because there was no money for motel rooms. Besides, they had a cow to get home.

I had no idea of what was happening or why. When we left, Heather was crying and told me how sorry she was but didn't know what else to do with her father getting weaker, her being away from home so much, and this might be better than going to an auction barn. She hoped I would be happy in my new home, but the tears continued to flow until the final hug goodbye.

I had no idea what it would feel like standing for 28 hours. No one offered me a drink. Each time a tire went flat, the weaving trailer scared me to death. Jim wasn't in very good spirits and slapped me on the butt trying to move me over to shift weight so he could change the tire. We stopped a few times for gas and so the children could use the bathroom. At least I had the advantage there, of not needing to be let out to relieve myself.

Being in the last stages of pregnancy, I was carrying extra weight. I was so relieved when we finally slowed and stopped after a bumpy driveway. It was late in the afternoon and everyone was exhausted. An old grizzled, weathered-looking human came up to the trailer and started laughing derisively, pointing at the trailer saying, "What the hell is that? Don't expect me to care for the damn thing!"

The kids spilled out of the camper and started running in every direction, trying to obtain a status report on their favorite animal. Jim yelled at his eldest son, "You get this cow in a corral. Give her water and hay. We'll let her rest tonight and put her in the pasture tomorrow. I guess we had better brand her. We didn't get a Bill of Sale."

I backed stiffly out of the cramped trailer. There was no ramp as I was used to. I stumbled stepping down and bruised one rear leg. I was led into the closest pen, where there was fresh cold water in a dented metal tank and I drank deep, long gulps. Another battered tank had grass hay in it, and I ate greedily. The corrals were in the sun with no shade or shelter and backed up to an old weathered barn. The fences were broken, and boards had been tied together and held with baling twine. There was no bedding, only dirt to lie down upon. I was so tired I picked the place most protected from the sun and dropped down on the bare ground. I quickly fell asleep and slept deep into the night.

Waking momentarily, I looked up to see more stars than I had ever noticed before in the moonless, clear, black sky. The wind was blowing. The air was not hot and muggy as it had been in Minnesota, but surprisingly cool and refreshing. I heard a coyote howling off in the distance. This was to be my new home.

I dreamed about Heather that night and the next, but as this was the next phase of my life I thought about the young life within me as I drifted back asleep.

Chapter 12

WESTERN LIFE

Someone was kicking my tail and telling me to get up. I had not met this human but instinctively knew we were not going to be friends. He reeked of alcohol. He had a long, ragged stick and was directing me to go into a squeeze chute. A whiff of smoke in the air detected something smoking red hot. The chute door dropped down behind me as I was forced to put my head into a small opening. This immediately triggered a heavy object to close around my head and keep me from moving. Was all this necessary? I was a gentle animal and had been trained to stand.

I saw the human approaching from the side and going toward my thigh with a red, hot glowing metal bar in his hand. He pressed it into my skin and held it there for several seconds. I screamed a moo and felt nauseated from the smell and feel of my flesh burning. A tear rolled down my face as I asked myself, "Am I to spend the rest of my life under these circumstances?" Then they opened the chute and prodded me to walk through.

"Get her up to the pasture with the pregnant mothers. We'll leave her there until she calves," the old man ordered brusquely.

Then Lorrie asked, "Do you think she'll have enough to eat? That pasture is pretty thin."

The response was, "She'll be fine. The pasture is still good."

"But..." Lorrie started.

The hired man broke in with, "No one has time to take care of a single cow." As the conversation ended, Lorrie walked toward the house, while I was pushed out to pasture.

My brand healed slowly, weeping and scabbing as scarred skin grew in. It cracked and bled as it dried and itched fiercely. Not even my tail could keep it free from flies. I loved being free to wander and sleep under trees. I discovered the pond where I could take a drink any time day or night. Birds ate beside me and even sat on my back picking at insects. The flies were unbearable, but there were no mosquitoes. That was a minor consolation.

The Eastern plains of Colorado are in an arid climate belt. By definition, "arid" means "excessively dry," having insufficient rainfall to support agriculture. This harsh environment is not for the faint of soul. The grassland ecosystem consists primarily of sagebrush, rabbit brush and snakeweed.

Giant ragweed grows eight feet tall. Grasses come up in limited quantities when there is rainfall, which isn't often. Poverty Brome, a tufted grass with barbed tops, grows nearly three feet tall. Downy Brome climbs to two feet tall in May and June. The state grass, Blue Granma, sprouts to two feet tall. Cattle prefer the grasses when they initially push through the soil and are tender. Gramma grass was a favorite when it matured because the heads were quite tasty. Cows grab these heads while walking, chomping and swallowing. Different species of grasses reaching peak maturity at slightly different times can keep the cattle in feed for about five months. This depends on seasons, rainfall, and the onset of the cold.

Looking over the plains, one sees thousands of acres of grasses swaying gently. Trees grow only along the creek beds, which are typically dry. The trees are mostly cottonwoods growing to one hundred feet tall. As magnificent as they appear, they are considered a weed and not useful for harvesting the wood, except to burn as firewood. These grand old trees with dead and broken branches accentuate the plains. Interspersed along the creek beds are a few willows and box elders, adding some variation to the otherwise desert plants of yucca, prairie rockets and grasses.

I was surprised to see any type of spring flowers in this environment fighting for space beside the yucca. Such a contrast from Minnesota pastures.

Again, I overheard children talking about the flowers as they rode in the truck bed with their parents to check on the cattle in the pasture. Looking back, I believe they were more interested in seeing the flowers than really checking on the condition of the cattle.

"It must be springtime again. Look!" exclaimed the oldest, who clearly had an interest in the flora and fauna of the area. "There are the Lance leaf Chiming Bells with delicate bluish flowers. These grow to be nearly twelve inches tall. A second early arrival is the Pasque flower belonging to the genus of plants named Anemone. These perennial herbs grow in windward climates and have white flowers. And look at the wild miniature roses! What a beautiful surprise on the prairie."

I got my nose pricked smelling these too vigorously in my never-ending pursuit of food. I was always famished. (Talk about working so hard, for so little).

He also talked about Indian Paintbrush which sprouted as moisture increased, poking through the hard soil with their vivid orange flowers. All of these plants were tenacious. The striking contrast of colors, unfolding and lying softly over the gentle landscape of the plains was peaceful in the spring, as this young man so eloquently stated.

I missed the type of feathered friends I was accustomed to at my old home with Heather. Colorado birds were strange by my standards. European starlings reminded me of the flowering trilliums in Minnesota just by their vast numbers. They flew everywhere, fighting for each insect as if it were the last. Their greenish-black feathers glimmered as they flew off, only a short distance, whenever they heard a noise. Immediately upon their return the squabbling would begin. These birds had beady eyes and a medium length sharp black beak. They are most helpful, however, during the late spring and early summer months when dusty miller moths hatch and they swoop and dive after these flying fuzzy morsels.

Doves nested in the grasses and perched on the barbed wire fences. They were plentiful and swarmed over the plains. Other common birds that survived on the plains were the Western Meadowlark, Lark Bunting and Cassin's sparrow. Meadowlarks would sit on the fences puffing out their bright yellow chest and chirping a melodious sound that carried over the valleys.

Hawks and barn owls sat on telephone poles by day and hunted in the evenings. The owls loved sneaking into the rancher's chicken coop and stealing chickens or pigeons. They could squeeze through such small inconspicuous holes in the fence that the humans never quite figured out how they disappeared.

There was a day in the heat of the summer when I noticed a bird I had never seen. One of the calves had died. As it was lying there being consumed by maggots, smelling foul, I noticed some very large birds circling overhead. Their wingspan was enormous, and I had never seen such creatures. Their heads were bare of feathers and bright red with long crooked beaks. There were many of them coming out of the sky. When the first one landed on the decaying carcass and tore flesh off the tiny dead creature, I was repulsed. Each of these prehistoric-looking birds took a turn at jumping onto the putrefying body and pulling off bites. Some tidbits were consumed on the spot, while larger pieces were torn free and swallowed in several gulps. Humans sometimes referred to these horrid scavengers as "Turkens" or "Turkey Vultures."

Sadly, the other cattle would not associate with me. I was different.

Cows demonstrate color prejudice quite noticeably and sort themselves to mingle with their own. Blacks like blacks. Spotted like spotted.

The isolation served my purpose these days, as I was always hungry. I grazed all day, late into the night and as the sun came up each morning, but I could not get filled up. As my baby within me grew larger, whatever I ate went to the development of the fetus inside me. My bones protruded more visibly with each passing day. I started eating weeds and licking brush; whatever I could find to eat. Drinking water helped fill the large reservoir of my stomach, but only temporarily.

No one came by any more to see how I was fending. It was assumed that a cow was a cow was a cow. Ranches were busy places. The children had quickly gone back to their normal routine. Lorrie liked to be in the house most of the time, when she was not at work in town. The feeding of the cattle was left to the men, and their assumption was that a milk cow was supposed to look bony.

My calving time approached. I had been through several births at my age. None of them were difficult, but I always had the strength to go through labor. Dairy cattle are allowed to dry up about three months before calving. I had been turned out in a big pasture with the beef cattle and allowed to forage, but no extra feed was provided. It turned out to be a bad decision where I was concerned. There was not enough food to sustain both me and my baby and I began losing weight.

One day Lorrie and two of her daughters were riding their horses through the pasture on their way to the upper holding pond. As they crested a hill looking down on the pasture, one of them pointed out something that looked like a dead cow lying underneath an old cottonwood tree. They galloped over, climbed off their horses and stared in disbelief.

The oldest gasped, saying, "Look! She is starving to death. Look at her bones! Why hasn't anyone noticed how thin she's been getting?"

Looking at me with sudden realization, tears welled up in Lorrie's eyes. "Oh my God, what have we done to you? We've got to get her up to the barn! Don't get back on your horses. We'll have to get her up and hope she'll follow us. Oh please, Marla, get up!" she begged.

With Lorrie and the girls pushing mightily, I attempted to rise several times on my rear legs by rocking back and forth. On the fifth attempt I raised halfway to the point of putting one front leg at a time under my body. Slowly, chewing my cud, I walked toward the barn as the humans surrounded me with encouraging voices and clucking their tongues.

Once in the barnyard Lorrie brought me some grain. It tasted delicious and I scarfed it all in a few mouthfuls. As I chewed, I raised my head, my neck stretched out and morsels fell from my grinding jaws onto the soil. Then I started eating the hay she had placed close to me. I ate hay until I felt quite full. Exhausted, I had to quit and lie down and rest. Lorrie came out and checked on me several times that night. Murmuring softly she apologized for not noticing my condition, promising to feed me better.

After supper, Lorrie brought Jim and all the children out to see me, reminding them of her earlier concerns about me having enough to eat on the arid range.

She said, "Dairy cows are different than beef cows. They need special care and much more food. This poor girl was used to lush knee-deep grass, not this sparse prairie grass. If we can't take care of her properly, we should sell her. She is so thin we should all be ashamed. We'll be lucky if she doesn't lose her calf."

Jim glared at Lorrie and the kids. "Dammit, I have a ranch to run! You were the ones that begged me to buy her. I have too much to do to be a nursemaid to an old skinny cow. It's your responsibility from here on out, so figure out what to do and get it done." Leaving them standing by the corral, he stormed back to the house.

Lorrie came out the next day and moved me to a pen with clean water near a decaying building that would provide some shade. Forking more hay into the feed bunk, and providing me some grain in a bucket, she came up to me scratching under my neck and talking softly, "I am so sorry, Marla. Please forgive us."

Two weeks later I had my baby. Though quite undernourished, my little brown bull calf was alive.

I was accustomed to my children being removed. This little guy was named Sam and he was brought twice a day to nurse. It was nice. He nuzzled softly and made feeble attempts to bunt. Lorrie came morning and night and milked me by hand, leaving just enough for my baby. Food was more plentiful, and I slowly gained weight. However, the birth had taken its toll. My age was starting to show.

Life on a ranch in Colorado was quite different from life on a farm in Minnesota. Seasons were not as harsh. Winters were typically warmer with only a few weeks of cold, but the wind blew relentlessly on the plains. One day temperatures peaked at 10 degrees but the next day they reached 50 degrees. The ups and downs caused animals to get sick because they could not adjust to the extreme fluctuations Treatments from the owners saved most but not all. In Minnesota when temperatures fell below zero our bodies adjusted. Thick hair coats developed and offered protection. Immune systems developed and were prepared.

In Colorado, spring came and grasses transitorily flourished, but pastures were not lush. Huge dumps of snow blew into March, April, and sometimes May. After a storm, it would warm and instantaneously start thawing. Some spring storms were bad enough to leave dead carcasses buried in drifts, but that was the exception, not the norm. The howling winds shifted the snow like sand on the sand dunes. Most range cows are left to forage in the winter, finding food and shelter when and where possible. In extreme cases, animals are supplemented with hay and minerals, especially as calving season approaches. By then the mothers need extra feed to build the milk supply and have the strength for the birthing process.

Because I was a dairy cow and frail for this range life, I was left in a corral able to get out of the wind, if it came from one of two directions. On one occasion, my corral was filled with snow drifted to the top of the fence. I survived in a small circle of mud, able to move a couple of feet as my body protected a small patch of ground underneath my belly. One of the humans would come and dig a path to the barn so I could get inside for grain and to be milked.

It was one of those springs with snow piled high, colder temperatures than usual and harsh northerly winds. I watched as two male humans saddled their horses, placed bandanas over their noses, and quickly rode off into the storm. "Maybe we can get to them before this gets worse. I hope we haven't waited too long. There are so many new calves. The coyotes are starving. They will be looking for an easy meal."

In a distant snow-encrusted pasture, a young bull calf named Joey was bawling loudly. It was pitch dark. He was only one month old, cold, wet and shaking with fear and misery. "Where did the herd go?" he asked as he woke from a very deep sleep. As the storm moved in, the cattle had drifted to the fence line, pushed by the fierce wind. He was without his mother, but not alone.

Jessica, a female calf, only a week older than Joey was also frightened but determined not to show it. "It was our fault. They told us to stay with the herd and not venture off. We fell asleep under this tree and they forgot we were here."

No mother looked back, because range cows instinctively knew that staying in the herd could mean life or death. "Stay close, keep up or be left behind." Those were the matriarch's exact words.

It was getting dark. In the near distance a silver streak slithered in the shadows. Not one, but three creatures were approaching. These were huge adult coyotes that had not eaten in several days. Salivating at the mere smell of flesh, they circled closer. Reversing directions, closing the gap, their frenzy continued to increase. Yelps and howls persisted, growing louder with each encircling movement. Joey didn't understand what was happening. Jessica sensed danger but was powerless to move. Her large beautiful eyes flashed with intense fear. One of the two calves uttered a soft cry: "Maaaa…Mother, help us!"

The rotating shadows became real bodies with snapping jaws and snarling teeth. Drool fell from the canine jaws and dripped onto tightly compressed snow. Joey bawled, letting out a loud cry. He took several steps backwards and bumped into Jessica. The two stood next to each other trembling. Intense fear prevented them from attempting to escape. With a sudden growl, the coyotes lunged at the calves. Jessica felt a sharp pain. It was excruciating. Powerful gripping jaws clamped around her throat. Blood squirted everywhere. "Oh Momma, where are you?"

she cried out. A second coyote grabbed Joey's throat, while another beast ripped open his abdomen. Guts spilled out on the ground. Both children died quickly. The food chain had entered yet another phase. The ravenous predators charged in, voraciously gorging themselves on the downed calves. Small bits of flesh and bone were scattered and buried into the snow, but small rodents and birds also scavenged for some nourishment.

The mother cows were some distance away, weak and unable to trek through the snowdrifts, preventing them from a rescue attempt. They repeatedly bellowed loudly, calling their young in the dark. As the screams subsided, so did their internal suffering. As the sounds faded into silence, they knew the struggle was over.

The cowboys never found the missing calves. Signs of the meal were concealed in shifting mounds of snow and with predators so hungry that every morsel was eaten. Droplets of blood were licked and swallowed with mouthfuls of snow. Bones were gnawed and crunched into bite sized pieces and devoured. The engorged coyotes slipped away under cover of darkness; their hunger satiated for the present.

Two days passed and the sun was bright, melting the snow with a vengeance. My pen quickly turned into knee-deep mud. As I stood, unable to move, chewing my cud with contentment, I knew someone would come to set me free. It would probably be the grumbling ranch hand. We had never formed a bond. He did what he was told but little else. In the meantime, I enjoyed the sun's warmth. After I was freed, I was moved to a small hillside. Someone came twice daily for the milking and grain. I always stood, well behaved. Heather's kindness remained with me. I was pushed and shoved, but never brutalized.

Foraging was work, especially after the initial tender grasses were eaten. In some of the pastures, we drank from rusty water tanks or little algae ponds. Shade was limited because trees were sparse. The sun mercilessly beat down on our bodies until it faded each evening. Sunsets and sunrises were generally quite spectacular- my favorite time of day. The evenings were surprisingly cool and refreshing.

Ranchers were a more diverse breed of human than farmers. Referred to as "cowboys", they wore wide brimmed hats, tall cowboy boots, generally with spurs and they chewed tobacco; spit on the ground at every opportunity. Most of them were just as angry as the farmers, just as filled with hostile emotions, ready to kick or hit anything and everything. These humans rode on horses to move the cattle. They knew how to throw a rope and to lariat their charges. They used spurs on their horses and rode them hard, but at least there was some type of bond between the man and his horse. Not so with us bovines.

One day I watched in horror as my son was roped, his feet tied as he was thrown hard to the ground. Then someone ran over with a red-hot piece of metal and held it on his tender young skin while smoke and the smell of burnt flesh permeated the air. As I had experienced, branding was a painful, disgusting process. But then the cattle that had horns had to have them snipped off. Dehorning was done with an odd-looking set of clippers which pinched the short horns off at the skin, then was daubed with a blood-stopping powder. In older calves with larger horns, the wound was cauterized with a hot iron to prevent bleeding, but the wounds brought hordes of flies, causing further misery to the animals. Immediately afterward, calves were given several vaccinations and the boys had their testicles cut off. When freed from the ropes the babies jumped up and ran bawling to their mothers and started frantically nursing which gave some measure of comfort and reassurance. When the job was completed, the gates were opened, the herd ran from the corrals and distanced themselves from the pain-provoking humans.

Some months later, the calves were weaned. Weaning was the process of taking the older babies away from their mothers. Screams and cries filled the air as calves and mothers were separated. Desperate cries filled the air for days. Babies, although weighing from 500-600 pounds, were panicked. No milk and no mother. Some became ill from the stress, though bunks filled with hay and water in troughs provided sustenance.

The weather during the summer was most interesting. The sky was cloudless, with vast arrays of different hues of blue that stretched for miles. On rare occasions darkened clouds formed with thunder rumbling loudly across the heavens. If it looked like rain, we all waited in jubilant anticipation. Clouds rolled by. Nothing. Not a drop. Then it was over, and the beautiful blue sky appeared again. When it did rain, the winds blew with such force that often the rain would come in horizontally and never touch the ground. Herds would gather in a circle with children in the middle, heads towards the center and backsides outward. Sometimes individuals stood by themselves with their tails to the wind, distanced from the herd. When it hailed, the hard-icy balls bounced painfully off our backs. Occasionally, they were large enough to leave welts and penetrating bruises.

It was interesting to observe new cattle from a distance. Newly placed bovines always surveyed the fence lines and discovered their boundaries. Some would go up to the barbed wire and sniff. Some were shy. Observing these new critters was gratifying, knowing they shared the same feelings of displacement I had felt.

Cows sniff a plant, reach down with mouth open and in one defining fraction of a second either grab it with their tongue or reject it. We wiggle our noses around weeds selecting only the best forage. Since we only have bottom teeth, it is necessary to force plants loose with firm tugs. As we graze, our ears hang perpendicular to our heads just like helicopter blades that are not in motion.

Invariably another, more aggressive animal will come up alongside and push their body into ours, just to show who the boss is. It is easiest to go on our way and leave them in your spot. Cows love to scratch. We bend nearly double to use our tongues to lick and scratch. Anything we cannot reach with our tongues, tails or hooves is rubbed against a tree, post or rock. It all feels good. It is only the areas that can't be reached that cause misery. Our tails are very busy in the summer. Swatting flies becomes a serious profession. The real problem occurs when the flies calculate the length of our tail and manage to sit just out of reach. One nice thing about rainstorms is that flies don't bother us. However, they don't take long to reassemble on our backs once the rain subsides.

Each day, in the morning and afternoon, we all form a single line and head off to the water when our thirst is greatest. The younger calves run and frolic. Elders walk with tranquil dignity. At the watering hole, there is jockeying for position. Sometimes as the frantic urges are at their highest, the roughness is serious and meaningful. Knocking anyone weighing less than yourself out of position and gaining your right for a drink is rewarded. Sometimes we stand, just momentarily, calculating if our stomachs will hold another swallow. Water drips from our lips. One at a time we drink, with the weaker animals waiting until the end when the slurping subsides. Now it is time for a nap, or perhaps time to go back to the pasture for more food.

Chapter 13

BITTERSWEET

I lived at this ranch on the plains of Colorado for two years before the twice daily milking became an unbearable chore for the busy family. I was hauled to the local auction and sold as a nurse cow. As it turned out, this was to be my last home. My new owners were ranchers, two women who were diversifying to find a way to make a living on their place. I was gentle and kind, loved babies, and fit into their program. This was an ideal placement, and I lovingly adopted and cared for four calves at a time, becoming the long-term mother I had always longed to be.

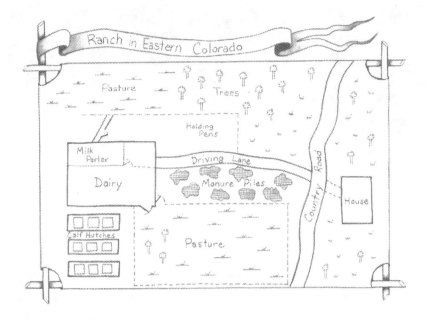

There were nine other cows already on duty feeding their babies. We each had our own shed and a small grassy meadow. The routine was different, but I was fortunate in that I learned quickly. With grain, anything was possible! For a week I was put in a chute twice daily. This initially raised all types of red flags of fear. I waited for the infliction of pain. My muscles twitched with apprehension. A small female human walked up and started brushing me. Then she brought me a large scoop of a corn mixture. She went to the other side and tore off the auction sticker, apologizing for pulling my hair coat. She was stronger than she appeared, with a tough, resilient air about her. She continued brushing until I had consumed all of the grain, and my skin felt invigorated. It brought back memories of my life with Heather in Minnesota. Then she went to a pen, opened a gate, and four baby calves came running over to my udder. I jerked backwards in the chute but was restrained by a stout metal pole blocking my exit. They started nursing, two of them bunting continuously, the third being slower and more gentle. The fourth couldn't find the teat and nursed under my stomach. He was turned around by the human and had the "faucet" placed in his mouth. He lost it three times before grasping on and suckling.

I noticed the two ornery calves were red with white faces, the gentle little guy was spotted black and white, but my favorite was the little brown one. He was my own kind, a Brown Swiss. After the calves sucked me dry, they were put back in their pen. The pole was pulled from behind me and I was gently persuaded to back out of the chute.

It was on the third day that I noticed all four of the calves smelled like me-like they were truly mine. I never knew until later that it took 72 hours for the scent of my milk to permeate the new babies. Once this transpired, they were my family and I let them nurse without being placed in the chute. I had fresh water, grain twice daily and lush new grasses. A newly built structure was erected for our protection. We even had two graceful, tall old cottonwood trees. Hours were spent under those trees in the shaded, cool air. It was a good life.

Other types of cows were purchased and brought home. I'll never forget a cow named Angel. She was called that because the human said she was so mean she hoped a nice name would change her disposition. It never happened. Angel hated babies. Even in the chute she would kick at them with her hind feet. Even squeezed tightly in the chute, she would find a way to harm the little creatures. Angel came to this place thin and starved. When she finally left, she was fat. Unfortunately, the kindness approach never worked and Angel had to be sold. If Angel had known her two choices; respond to the kindness or be sold again, perhaps she would have chosen more wisely. Ignorant of her fate, the cow was hauled back to the auction.

Another cow named Sugar was my neighbor. She was in a pasture many times larger than mine with nine young heifers. Sugar was dried up but was placed in the pasture to lead and protect the youngsters. They stuck like glue to Sugar's side. At first the night noises of the owls and coyotes scared them. During the day storms and winds frightened them.

They needed to learn, and Sugar taught them well. She initially tried to be indifferent, but the closeness grew throughout the summer. Wherever Sugar roamed, her group trailed faithfully behind.

One day one of the youngsters with Sugar started to develop a very sore foot. It developed into a nasty case of foot rot and proceeded to worsen. Two humans came out in a truck with medicine and a lariat. For over an hour they tried to rope the heifer so the lariat could be tossed over its head. These women were not cowgirls and had never been trained to rope an animal. It was very frustrating for them, because each time the cornered animal sidestepped just in time to miss the noose.

Sugar stayed on the periphery and watched. It was sad and amusing at the same time. She knew the heifer was in pain, and she couldn't fix it. She knew she was scared but needed help. What could she do? Sugar walked to the outside of the heifer and firmly pushed her towards the human with the rope. Another throw and they missed again. One more time, Sugar went to the outside of the heifer and nudged her toward the human with the rope. This time the rope soared over its head and securely settled around her neck.

The heifer bolted as the human held onto the rope. Sugar walked slowly over to the sidelines watching; there was nothing more she could do. The second human ran over to the end of the rope and grabbed on with both hands. It took both of them to hold onto the frightened, plunging animal.

Slowly they narrowed the distance between them and the beast. One last pull and they snugged the rope around the trailer hitch on the truck.

Once the animal was secure, treatment began. The frightened animal only glared at Sugar, unappreciative of her helpfulness. A large syringe filled with antibiotics was taken out of the truck as well as some antiseptic spray. The heifer suffered one last indignity of an injection in her neck and purple spray on the bottom of its sore foot. As the rope loosened, she ran over to Sugar for consolation. Sugar glanced in my direction as if to say, "What's a mother to do?"

One morning as we were resting in our pen after everyone had finished their breakfast, we heard a tremendous racket on the dirt road below the farm. Curious, everyone got up and went over to the fence to see what was going on. Coming up the road was a huge herd of black cattle of all ages and sizes. They were bawling and trotting right up the middle of the thoroughfare. Humans on horseback were in the lead and following up the rear. Dust clouded the sky as far as we could see. Finishing chores, our human looked up and exclaimed, "Oh look! A cattle drive! Can you believe in this day and age they still take their cows to pasture by herding them with horses? Isn't it wonderful? Reminds me of all the stories I have read about the Old West. What are they going to do when they come to the "T" in the road? There's an open pasture gate there!"

No need to worry. Two of the humans on horseback slowly eased their way into the roadside ditch and walked past the herd to block the routes they did not want the herd to take. Some of the cattle tried to get around, but the majority followed the proper course up another mile to the pasture where they would spend the summer. Continuing to watch, our entertainment for the day, we noticed a truck slowly following behind the herd, along with another horse and rider. They stopped and picked up the stragglers--calves that were too small to keep up with the herd. These calves were tied and placed in the bed of the truck, then hauled to the final destination. The noise of bawling cattle was deafening: mothers and babies calling frantically because they had lost each other, confused youngsters wailing because this was their first herd drive, and the bulls were just angry at everyone because their family was separated. The line of cattle extended for nearly a mile.

We stayed along the fence line until the last of the old cows passed over a hill and out of sight. It was quite a spectacle, and one I would never forget.

Then the spring storms came. This year, that meant a deluge of rain. Due to the dampness and temperatures going from very warm to very chilly, many of our baby calves became ill with "scours". This was a deadly form of watery discharge called diarrhea, as I heard the veterinarian explain. Scours are usually caused from bacteria or a change in weather or purchasing calves at an auction where their exposure was intensified. Calves at the auction did not always get the colostrum from their mothers because they were just going to be sold. The mortality rate for these babies was extremely high and suffering before the finality of death was horrible for the owners and charges. The sick babies squirted fluid out of their backsides that unfortunately contained nutrients. Little bodies could not live very long unless this was stopped. Their bodies dehydrated. The weaker ones soon could not stand up to nurse. Looking gaunt and depressed, their eyes sank back in their heads and, emaciated, they died. Despite trying many cures including antibiotics and homemade concoctions to keep the food in, many of the calves died.

The humans often wept as they lifted up the frail, lifeless cadavers. Laying them gently in the truck bed for removal to the "dead pile," one agonized saying, "Why do we do this? We can barely make a living raising these babies, and I hate it when we lose one!"

The other replied, "Remember what David, our neighbor, said. He calculated that with raising cattle his hourly wage was less than 10 cents. The pain of watching these calves die is not worth that. I guess we have to think of the good times, but that sure isn't now. These babies deserve better. They are so frail and die so easily. If the dairies had only cared enough to give them their colostrum when they were born..." she lamented.

The next week some of the surviving animals were loaded into the trailer and hauled to the auction. Once again, as the humans were relating the events to each other we noticed more frustration. "Can you believe the one day of the week we chose to go to the auction, the rains washed out the roads? I'm surprised we made it back home safely, what with the trailer sliding from side-to-side on the muddy roads! If we hadn't stopped awhile and waited for things to dry up a bit, I think we would have ended up in the ditch. It was awful! This sure is a hard way to make a living. The good news is that when it rains most of the ranchers are at the sale and we get higher prices."

Chapter 14

FULL CIRCLE

Finally, spring eased into a mild summer with abundant crops due to the earlier wet months. Trucks brought load after load of hay to the farm, ensuring adequate feed during the cold winter months ahead. We contentedly grazed in the fields, our babies growing strong beside us. Despite occasional severe summer storms bringing rain and hail accompanied by fierce gusty winds and lightning storms, no livestock losses occurred.

Our lives settled into a calm routine with little stress and the farm prospered. The women sometimes took the weaned calves and loaded them into the trailer, taking them to auction. They returned with more young calves and occasionally a new nurse cow. As they adjusted to each other, the new mothers and babies joined us in the pasture.

A mild fall followed, and fences, sheds and outbuildings were repaired by the industrious women as they prepared for another winter on the plains. The tractor was also kept busy, cleaning out the pens that were out in pasture, with the pile of manure behind the barn growing each day. Their work never seemed to stop, yet they seemed happy and sometimes we could hear them laughing and talking as they went about their daily chores.

It was not until early winter that we noticed more activity than usual.

A mother named Paula, down three pens from mine, was never friendly. In fact, she was totally antisocial and ran to the other end of her pen whenever the humans approached. She was due to have her baby, but was late and the snow was early. There was a drainage ditch running through her pen.

One night very late we saw something bright moving toward us in the dark. Everyone bolted to the other end of their pen. Lights after dark scared us. It was the humans with a flashlight, coming to do a night check on the expectant mothers before going to bed. Paula had calved a few minutes earlier, but had her baby in the ditch filled with water and snow.

The humans shined the light over the pen when they happened to see a calf's head with nostrils flaring, come up for air. Together they jumped over the fence and splashed into the freezing water, searching to find the submerged body. Paula stood nearby watching with great internal turmoil. Part of her wanted to run, but the other part knew her baby was in trouble. She knew she could not help, and her only recourse was to let the humans save her child.

With the two women struggling mightily, at last the calf's limp body was pulled from the water. It was not breathing. One of the shivering ladies blew repeatedly into the nostrils and pushed rhythmically on the chest cavity. The little body moved, having been just seconds from death. They grabbed the baby and tucked it under the fence, one turning to Paula saying, "I know you don't like us and I don't know why, but you must trust that we will try to save your baby." Paula didn't understand the words, but she sensed the humans were going to help. Cold, exhausted, and panting, the calf was quickly carried into the warmth of the house. We were told later about something called a bathtub and warm water. Oh yes, and something else called whiskey, carefully poured down the struggling calf's throat, which helped revive the little guy.

The next morning the now-lively small creature was brought back to its mother's corral. Paula ran away but then halted, curious and hopeful that this was her baby and it was all right. She came back, nuzzled her baby as it scrambled over to her, and moved into position to start nursing. The women, feeling courageous, reached out to pet the mother. Paula flinched ever so slightly at the gentle touching, but never ran away again. She realized they were there to help. They had saved her child, and she would not forget their kindness.

The rest of the winter was uneventful for me, my foster children and the herd in general. It was a mercifully mild winter, with mostly normal snowfall and very few blizzards. We were warm in our sheds with our babies, and well cared for. For the first time in my life, I was not able to become pregnant, and my aging bones creaked and popped as I moved. Arthritis and pain accompanied me.

One evening toward spring, as I was watching the stars, I counseled my babies telling them I would be leaving soon, and they would be alone. "Be brave my children. You can trust these humans. They will treat you well."

Birds began chirping as the sun peaked up over the eastern plains the next morning. Life for the others would continue but curled gracefully underneath the aged cottonwood tree next to the shed, Marla did not wake up. Her babies were frantic with hunger, but afraid to be close to the still form on the ground. Something was not right.

The women wept as they found her and moved her babies into a pen with another nurse cow. This time instead of moving her by tractor to the dead pile, they dug a deep grave close to the old cottonwood and gently placed her there where she would rest in peace, with respect for the life she had lived.

Marla had gone to be with her mother at last.

ABOUT THE AUTHORS

Diana R. Wright, was uprooted at the age of ten when her father hustled a reluctant wife and five children in pursuit of his dream to be a Minnesota dairy farmer. The harsh farm life, weather and family circumstances led Diana to bond deeply with her bovine charges. Her involvement in youth 4-H included exhibiting and demonstrations emphasizing care and good husbandry. She has spent a lifetime studying cow behaviors, has a degree in Biological Science and is a certified AI technician. She advocates that all beings have feelings and need nurturing. They deserve "creature comforts."

"Marla" is Diana's second book. To know more about this author read "Too Damn Dumb to Think" a memoir published by Bedazzled Ink Publishing, which received a Rainbow Award Honorable Mention, and available through Amazon.

Rita J. Cayou, was fascinated by cows from an early age. She had "dairying" relatives and the placidity she experienced in those creatures gave them a special place in her heart. At eighteen she got a job wrangling horses and helping with a small herd of beef cattle. Years later she moved to Elbert, Colorado and for the next 18 years, she and her family were involved in 4-H, raising both beef and dairy cattle. For years she hand-milked providing fresh milk to her family.

Owning neighboring ranches in Elbert for a time, Diana & Rita shared experiences and wisdom regarding their charges. Hence the collaboration on this book.

Printed in the United States
by Baker & Taylor Publisher Services